MW00943458

Orphan Train Bride

by Teresa Ives Lilly

Copyright 2012

All rights reserved as permitted under the U.S.
Copyright Act of 1976. No part of the publication may
be reproduced, distributed or transmitted in any form or
by any means, or stored in a database or retrieval
system, without the prior permission of the publisher.
Lovely Romance Press

Cover Photo by Shelby Lilly
Cover Model Shelby Lilly
Cover Design by: Shera Lilly Lopez

Chapter 1

Kelli Martin gazed out the train window, at the town of Emporia, Kansas, as the brakes locked and the black giant slowly made its way towards the small wooden platform of the station. Emporia was much like all the other towns the train had passed through on the long journey from New York. It looked a very pleasant place, as far as Kelli could tell from this view. Kelli sighed, *I only hope that a miracle will occur in this town.*

As the train slowed and came to a stop, Kelli glanced out the window and noticed a wagon heading into town. She leaned over so she could see better. She quickly noted that there was nothing special about this particular wagon, so she wondered what had caught her attention in the first place. Then she saw the driver. It was obvious what had caused her to take a closer look; the golden streaks of his hair glistened in the bright Kansas sun.

He was a very large, young man, with hair the color of the wheat she had seen waving on the prairie, as the train moved through the plains. It too had glittered in the sun. Kelli pressed closer to the window.

"Whoa!" the man called to his horses and the huge beasts came to a stop beside the train. Then the handsome man jumped down from the wagon and sidled up beside one of the sturdy horses. He bent over and picked up one of the horse's legs so he could inspect its hoof. Kelli saw him pull a knife out of his pocket and use it to pull a stone out of the hoof. Then he patted the mare's leg, stood back up, and turned slightly. His eyes suddenly locked with Kelli's because he was standing right beside the window that she had her face pressed against.

When he saw her, he broke into a smile. Kelli's face flushed red, ashamed that the giant of a man had noticed her staring at him.

It was hard not to stare though. In all her life at the New York Orphanage, she had never before seen any young man as large and as bronze as this man.

It must be from working out in the sun, Kelli decided.

The man's smile stretched across his face. After a second, he took off his Stetson and gave a slight bow to her.

"Ma'am!"

Kelli couldn't help herself. She smiled back at him. She timidly lifted a small gloved hand and quickly waved. The man bounded back into his wagon and clicked the reins, causing the horses to move on. Kelli sat back against the hard seats, feeling the heat in her cheeks.

Now that was a true cowboy, she thought. *Just like the ones I've read about in my penny novels. I would love a chance to talk to him, to find out more about his life...* Kelli laughed at herself. There was no point in thinking about things that would never come true. Her life was in New York, teaching in the orphanage where she had grown up. There was never going to be a chance for her to meet this cowboy or any other cowboy for that matter.

"Whatcha thinking about, Kelli?" Charlie, a small waif asked, as he clambered onto nineteen year old Kelli's lap, interrupting her thoughts. For a moment she felt a wave of disappointment knowing that she would never see the golden cowboy again, but holding the small child in her lap reminded her of her duty; to get Charlie adopted in this town.

4

Charlie was small for a seven year old, and because of the metal cage he wore on his leg, it wasn't surprising that he had not been adopted yet. The nuns had not wanted to put Charlie on the Orphan Train because the Children's Aid Society requested that only healthy, white children be sent. Kelli, who had been assigned the job of taking care of all the children during the weeks on the Orphan Train, begged the nuns to allow Charlie to come along because she could not bear to leave the boy behind. She had raised him since birth. Charlie was like her own child and she wanted him to have a better chance at life.

Unfortunately, in each town where the Orphan Train stopped, whenever a potential adoptive parent noticed his leg, they quickly passed him by. Many people wanted healthy children as extra farm hands, but even those who wanted children they could love, also wanted a child who could do chores. Because they did not know what Charlie's abilities were, they doubted the small boy, with the cage on his leg could do any real work, so they never chose him.

Kelli knew that Charlie could do many things, but she also understood that farmers probably were afraid to take the chance.

"Oh, I'm just remembering the things that my mother used to tell me." Kelli looked into the young boy's face and smiled. She did not want Charlie to guess she had been daydreaming about the golden cowboy.

"About God always being with you, and always having a good plan for your life?" Charlie asked, wisdom shining in his eyes. Kelli gave a little tickle to his sides. Charlie squealed. *He is such a wonderful little boy. Those families don't know what they have passed by.*

"Yes, I've been reminding myself of the things my mother always told me about God, because I've been feeling lonely, especially as the other children have left the train and found new homes."

"Me too," Charlie added, a tear hovering in the corner of his eye. The boy gruffly swiped his sleeve across his face. Kelli wrapped her arms around him and remembered.

Charlie had been brought to the orphanage a week after Kelli arrived. He was just a few days old. Kelli fell in love with him and spent as much time caring for him as she possibly could. Over the years, the nuns turned Charlie's care completely over to Kelli.

Now that the Orphan Train trip was nearly over, and Charlie had not been adopted, Kelli wished she had not insisted he be given the chance to ride on the train. She hated to think about the way that Charlie would be taunted by the boys, when he returned to the orphanage. Especially by the older boys who had not been given a place on the train because Charlie had been sent instead.

Still, she was glad in a way that Charlie had not been adopted. She really did not know if she could handle saying good-bye to him.

"Kelli, I'm not going to get adopted am I?" The young boy's voice quivered as he looked deeply into her eyes for an honest answer.

Kelli did not want to make promises that might not come true. "We have to wait and see what God's plan for you is. If God wants you to be adopted, you will be. If not, then we will go back to New York together and we will have had this great adventure to tell everyone about."

Charlie rested his head in the crook of her arm and nodded. "Okay Kelli, but it sure would be nice to live out here in a place with lots of land, and cows and pigs and stuff." His eyes traveled to the window.

"Yes, Charlie, it would be." Kelli longed to live in the country now that she had seen it. New York was crowded and filthy, and she had no hope of ever making a home for herself there as long as she worked at the orphanage.

Unfortunately, there were no other jobs that she was qualified for. Kelli was keenly aware that she would end up living and working in the orphanage for most of her life. She would also become an old maid there because life in an orphanage meant no hope of ever meeting a young man; especially not a bronzed cowboy.

Kelli turned to look out the window again. She could no longer see the cowboy or his wagon. Suddenly, a wild thought filled her mind. *What if I were to stay in this town? What if I were to get a job in one of the shops along the boardwalk?* Kelli sat up again and pressed her face against the window, allowing her eyes to travel up and down the wooden walkway, scrutinizing the variety of businesses.

They all look so inviting. Kelli's mind raced for a minute with the idea, until she remembered that she had no skills that would allow her to stay in the town. Her only training was taking care of babies and teaching small children. Even though she taught at the orphanage, she had no formal training, so she could never hope to get hired in this town as an official teacher.

Kelli shrugged back into the seat. She hated to admit it, but tomorrow she would have to go back to New York. She would never get to live in the country, or travel west again.

These thoughts made her heave a heavy sigh. She looked down at the small boy snuggled up beside her. He was another reason she had to go back to New York. She could never leave Charlie alone.

The young boy looked up at his beloved teacher. She wondered if he could see the troubled look in her eyes. He always seemed able to sense her thoughts.

"Maybe I'll get adopted in this town, Kelli," Charlie assured her. "And if I do, I'll ask them to adopt you too! I don't want to go to a new home without you."

Kelli laughed at the child's serious sincerity. She hugged him tightly. His innocent hope brought a small rush of tears to her eyes. She adjusted herself on the stiff seat so that Charlie could lay his head on her lap. When he was settled, she began to sing to him.

******

Kelli had barely finished one song when Sister Marter, the Matron who accompanied Kelli and the group of fifty orphans from New York, suddenly appeared before her.

"Come along, it's time to go." The nun reached over, picked up her small satchel, and turned in a brisk fashion. She was used to being obeyed, so she never looked back to see if Kelli was following. Instead, she made her way towards the front of the coach.

Kelli shook Charlie's shoulders to wake him. The young boy sat up, rubbing his eyes. He noticed Sister Marter leaving the train.

"Come along Charlie." Kelli pulled a small comb out of her pocket and ran it through his hair. Charlie glanced out the window again and took a great gulp.

Kelli looked down at Charlie. He stood up straight and gave a trembling smile. Kelli could see that he was nervous. His face was pale and his bottom lip quivered. She guessed that he was worried he would not get adopted in this town either, or that if he did get adopted, he would have to leave her behind.

Kelli took Charlie's hand and squeezed it reassuringly as they stepped down from the train. Sister Marter walked ahead of them. She stepped into the small train depot office to ask exactly where they were supposed to go.

Kelli and Charlie stood quietly waiting for Sister Marter, each one looking the town over with tired eyes, both lost in their own thoughts. At first, Kelli thought that this town was like all the others, but on closer inspection, she decided that this particular town looked very interesting. She wished there was time to stroll the wooden boardwalk, before she had to hustle Charlie into a building, where he would be inspected by a group of prospective parents.

Suddenly Kelli sensed something different about this town. There were several people walking along the wooden walkways, in front of the buildings on the street, but Kelli saw no crowd of people huddled together outside any of the buildings, waiting to see the orphans, as there had been in the other towns. Kelli spun around, squinting as she looked up and down the row of buildings again.

Just then, Sister Marter stepped out of the small office, and Kelli could see the strained look on her face. It was obvious she was very upset.

"What is wrong, Sister?" Kelli watched the older woman stride towards them and stop in a huff.

"Well, something has gone wrong," the nun announced angrily. "This town was not notified at all about the Orphan Train coming. There was no ad put in their paper, and no fliers put up around town!"

"You mean, no one knows we are here?"

"That's exactly what I mean. I was also told that the council has not yet decided if they want to allow an Orphan Train to stop in their town, so they are unwilling to even make an announcement about us being here now."

"But this is our last stop." Kelli's eyes fell on the small boy in sympathy.

"Yes, I know," Sister Marter acknowledged. "There is nothing I can do about it. They told me that they would consider being put on the list the next time an Orphan Train comes this way, but even then, they would want more than one child to choose from."

******

Charlie had been absorbed in watching several horse drawn buggies pass by so he had not heard the conversation between Sister Marter and Kelli. When he looked up and noticed Kelli's gentle but sad smile, his heart plummeted. He moved closer to Kelli and slipped his hand back into hers.

Kelli held back her own tears.

"I'm not going to get adopted here, am I, Sister?" The boy's tiny shoulders slumped.

Sister Marter tried to smile. Charlie was the only boy in the whole orphanage who could break through her cold and normally rigid stance.

"I'm sorry dear," she spoke in a gentle voice, which not many of the orphans ever had a chance to hear. "There has been a mix up and no one even knows you are here. It is too bad, but we will all have to begin our journey back to New York tomorrow."

Kelli noted the sag in Charlie shoulders, but when he turned his eyes towards her again, she was amazed at his brave face.

"At least we get to stay together, Kelli. It must be what God wants."

Kelli turned away for a moment to wipe her eyes. This child was stronger than she was. He relied on God more than she did.

Kelli's voice cracked. "Yes, Charlie, it must be what God wants."

"We will stay in the hotel tonight," Sister Marter announced. The three of them gathered their few bags together and started down the walk way towards the hotel. Sister Marter marched ahead quickly. Both Kelli and Charlie scurried behind, trying to keep up with her, but their eyes kept darting back and forth, trying to see everything possible and hoping not to miss a single detail of the town. Charlie pointed out several businesses including the Proctor General Merchandise Store.

Kelli allowed her eyes to trail up and down the street, hoping to catch one more glimpse of the tall, young cowboy again, but his wagon was nowhere to be seen.

When they reached the hotel, Sister Marter pushed open the wooden door and moved towards the front desk to secure a room. Charlie and Kelli hung back.

"I wish I could have been adopted in this town," Charlie told Kelli. "It looks real nice."

Kelli's heart ached for the same thing. The town looked so inviting; there was quite a variety of businesses along the main street. She wanted to be able to explore them all. Kelli knew that they would be in this town for only a short time, but perhaps, if she could get a chance to look around, there would be some type of work she could do in this town. If she were able to find a job, she might be able to keep Charlie with her.

Too quickly, Sister Marter called for them to follow her into the hotel. Kelli and Charlie trudged unhappily up the stairs and down the long hallway behind Sister Marter. When they had settled in the room, Sister Marter suggested they all take a rest. Charlie claimed that he wasn't a bit tired, but he fell asleep quickly once he was tucked into the bed.

Kelli lay quietly on the small sofa in the room, but she did not close her eyes. Instead, she waited until she could hear the even breathing that indicated that Sister Marter was asleep as well. Then Kelli inaudibly slipped off the sofa, stepped out of the room, and hurried down the stairs. She made her way to the front desk.

The front desk clerk looked up as she approached. "Can I help you?"

"Yes, I was wondering how I could find out if there are any jobs available in this town?"

"You're very young ain't you?" the man stated and then asked, "ain't you one of the orphans that just came in?"

Kelli was surprised that he knew about the Orphan Train since no one had been prepared for them, but she assumed that just as in any small town, news traveled fast here.

"Yes, I am, but I'm not that young. I am nineteen and have been working in the orphanage most of my life."

Kelli lifted a stubborn chin when she spoke. "I guess you ain't so young after all." He eyed her more closely. He ran his tongue over his lips and smiled in such a way that caused Kelli to shudder in distaste.

The man thought for a moment, and then suggested that she go to the general store. "There might be some notices hanging on the wall there. That's where everyone posts notices when they want to hire someone," he explained. "If it had been last week, I would have hired you myself. I just got a new cleaning girl yesterday."

"Oh, I'm sorry I missed the chance," Kelli answered, actually glad the job working for this man, was no longer available. She did not like the way he looked at her. Kelli had little experience around men, but the feeling she got when this man boldly looked her up and down, told her that there was something rather sinister about him. "I will take your advice and run over to the general store right now."

Kelli rushed out the front door and turned in the direction of the general store. She tried not to run, but found that her feet were flying. She knew that she had very little time before Sister Marter and Charlie would waken, notice her missing, and come after her. This was the only chance she might ever have to find a job, so she hurried along.

13

When Kelli pushed open the door, she could tell that the general store was empty, except for the old man working behind the counter. He barely lifted his head when she walked in. For a few moments Kelli just stood in the middle of the store looking around wide eyed. She had not been in a store for years, at least not since before her parent's death when she was twelve.

Kelli's eyes lit with interest, enthralled with everything she saw. She wandered around, lightly running her hand over the new and unusual items. There were all sorts of things that she had never seen before: odd tools hanging from the ceiling, jars filled with wonderful looking candy on the counter and several bolts of a light material that were labeled 'Calico'. Kelli wished she could own some of the calico material to make herself a new dress; a light dress, unlike the uniform she had to wear in the orphanage.

Kelli looked down at the serviceable gray dress that she wore. It had been given to her to wear during the Orphan Train trip and she was expected to make it last for a year or more. There was no point dreaming about something she could not have. This dress, and the other old gray one she owned, were enough for any orphan girl.

Finally satisfied that she had seen everything, Kelli stepped up to the counter and cleared her throat to get the old man's attention. He was busy looking over a list of numbers, so it took several seconds before he looked up at her. By the look on his face, Kelli could see that he was obviously irritated by her presence.

"Can I help you?" the man nearly barked at her. Kelli stepped back slightly, frightened by his tone, but she knew how important her task was, so she shook off the fear.

"I was wondering…I mean…I was looking for…well the gentleman at the hotel told me that there was a place here where jobs were posted," she finally squeaked.

"You're a bit young for a job ain't you?" the man growled. He gazed at her for a second, snorted and turned away.

Embarrassed, Kelli felt like slinking away, but she knew that this was her only chance, so she moved a step closer to the counter.

"I'm nineteen, almost twenty and I need a job," she spoke up clearly, in the voice she had used on the train to control the children.

The man glanced up when he heard the authoritative sound of her voice. He stared at Kelli with more interest. "I guess you do look old enough after all, but what does your Ma think about you getting a job? Shouldn't you be settling down and getting married?"

"I'm an orphan," Kelli stated, chin up.

"Oh, well," the man stumbled over his words. Kelli could tell that he didn't know what to say about that. It was always awkward for people because most of them had never heard of an orphan as old as Kelli before. In most people's minds, orphans were just little kids.

"Where'd you come from?"

Kelli was frustrated, and tired of explaining her presence. "I was on the Orphan Train that just pulled in to the station about an hour ago."

"Orphan Train! Orphan Train? Never heard of such a thing."

Kelli felt angry. She had little time to find a job and this man was wasting precious minutes.

"Can you please just tell me if you have a place where jobs might be posted?"

The man stared at her for another moment, then pointed across the room. "There are some posts hanging up on the wall over there, behind that shelf. Go have a look. Can't say there will be anything there for a girl."

Kelli moved quickly towards the wall where the man had indicated the posts were. Her heart was pounding with excitement, but once she reached the notices her expectations were quickly dashed. There were very few posts at all, and those that hung, pell-mell on the board, only offered jobs for young men. She thought that maybe she could convince someone to hire a woman instead of a man if she found an appropriate ad, but there were no jobs that she felt she could fulfill.

There was one post offering men a job working on the railroad but Kelli did not think she would be able to do that. There were several ads posted by farmers, offering room and board to bachelors for a small fee. Kelli imagined that this was one source of income for a farmer, but it wouldn't help her.

She scanned the board again. Unfortunately, there was not one post or ad indicating a job for a woman. Kelli's hope began to fade. If she could not find a job, she would have to get on the morning train and travel back to the orphanage. There was little chance that she would ever get to leave the orphanage again, so she would never be able to find a job anywhere else; especially not in the country. A tear slipped down her face.

Busy in her musing, Kelli did not notice that someone else had entered the store. As she stood brokenhearted, Kelli suddenly heard a new voice speaking. Another man was talking to the gruff store owner.

"Good morning, Mr. Joslin." Kelli heard a much younger man say. She did not want anyone to see that she was crying so she pushed herself further back into the corner, until she was hidden behind the shelf and could not be observed.

Through the slats in the shelves she could see that the younger man was the golden cowboy she had seen from the train window earlier. Kelli couldn't bear for him to see her crying like a silly school girl. She wiped her eyes with her sleeve and stood silently, listening as the two men spoke.

"Howdy, Carter, you need some supplies?" the store owner asked. The young man's voice was rather loud and Kelli couldn't help hearing his answer.

"Yes, I am here to pick up some supplies," he handed a list to the store owner. "And I was wondering if there was any mail for me?" The young man tried to drop his voice to a whisper but Kelli could still hear him. He looked around furtively, as if afraid someone would overhear his conversation.

His behavior intrigued Kelli, so she moved closer to the back of the shelving where she was able to hear and see the man more clearly.

Now that she could see him at such close range, she could tell that although he was young, he was older than her. Kelli was once again amazed at what a muscular build he had.

The sunlight that snuck through the window at the front of the store lit the area he was standing in enough that Kelli could see that his golden blonde hair waved gently around his face.

Her mouth gaped open for a second as she stared at him. Although she had not seen many men in all her years at the orphanage, her experience, having been limited to orphan boys, the milk man, the priests and the occasional husband who came with their wife to look at the orphans, she could not help but feel once more that this was the most handsome man she had ever seen.

He was tall and strong and his skin was tan. From her vantage point, Kelli could see his face, which was clean shaven and made him look very young. She noticed that there seemed to be a touch of sadness in his eyes though. *What could make such a handsome man look so sad?*

"No mail for you today, Carter," the old man snickered. "Hoping to hear back from that mail order bride ad you put out in the city paper?"

Red flashed across the young man's cheeks. Kelli could tell that the old haggard man was purposely trying to embarrass the younger man. She felt a surge of sympathy for him, but at the same time she wanted to hear his answer. She had heard that men in the West sometimes posted ads looking for women to come from the East to marry them. She couldn't help but wonder why someone as good looking as Carter would need a mail order bride.

The young man looked around to see if anyone had over heard the man's comment. He could not see Kelli behind the shelf but she still pulled back a bit. When he decided that the store was empty, he answered. "Well, yes I was."

Carter sighed. There was no point in trying to hide anything in this town. The store owner knew everything about everyone in town and loved to share his knowledge with anyone who would listen.

"Seems like a foolish thing to me. Can't imagine any decent woman wanting to come clear out here to Kansas to get married to a perfect stranger."

"It seems that way," Carter agreed. "I've waited three months already and haven't heard from even one woman." Carter shook his head. "I might as well just give that idea up."

"Why don't you just marry one of the women from around here? They already know all about the hardships of life on the prairie. Even if you did get some woman to come here from the city, she probably wouldn't be able to stand the prairie life. You know city women ain't used to the long, lonely winters we have here."

Carter smiled softly at the man's words, but he merely shook his head.

"There is no one out here that I love, and no one who loves me." Carter laughed, and Kelli noted that there was a bitter tone to it.

"Love! Who has time for such silliness? You need a wife. Seems to me that any one of the single women around here should do. Besides, you wouldn't love a stranger from the city either."

Carter was silent for a moment. Kelli had been holding her breath while the two men spoke. She slowly let it out and quietly gulped in more air.

After a few seconds, Carter shrugged his shoulders. "That is true. I suppose anyone will do, but I was hoping not to have to choose from the ladies in this town. None of them have really shown much interest in me, especially in my situation. Most of the single woman are either very young or much older than me."

"That's sure; babies or widows. I still think that one of them would jump at a chance to marry you though. I'm know Miss Lila would."

Carter cringed. Miss Lila Aderson was the only woman in the area who had made it perfectly clear that she would marry him, but she was already thirty five and Carter found her to be a bit too bossy for him. However, she was the one neighbor he trusted to help him.

"I might have to rethink the whole thing. I may even have to put an ad in the New York Times."

"Wouldn't that be something," the old man slapped his knee. "A real New York lady coming all the way to Kansas to marry a farmer."

Carter tried to shake the picture out of his mind. It did sound pretty crazy.

Just then a woman, with two small boys tagging behind her, marched into the store and began to shop. Not wanting to miss out on a sale, the store owner picked up Carter's list to hurry him along.

"Well, maybe next week you'll get a letter."

Carter looked over his shoulder to see if the woman was paying attention to their conversation. He sighed with relief when he realized she had not heard the man's comment.

"You want me to fill this order now or just have it all sent out to you?"

"Fill it now. I have some other things to do in town, but I will come back for it. My buckboard is sitting out front." Carter turned and headed out the door.

Kelli stood still for another moment. She was astounded at what she had just heard. She could hardly believe that the golden cowboy could possibly need to put an ad in a paper to get a wife. She shook her head in wonder, then suddenly a thought entered her mind. To her own amazement, she stepped out from behind the shelf, and without any hesitation, hurried towards the door.

She was so intent on her mission that she did not acknowledge the store owner when he asked, "Did you find any kind of job?"

Kelli pushed open the door, rushed out without looking where she was going and slammed right into Carter's back. He had stopped outside the door to read over a list he held in his hand.

"Oh, excuse me, Miss," Carter said kindly, turning to see who had bumped into him. Kelli was glad that his voice did not register any irritation. But she was embarrassed that she had slammed into him.

"I'm really sorry, it was my fault," Kelli stammered.

Carter smiled. "Nothing to fret about, Miss."

For a second he wondered who the girl was. There was something familiar about her, but he could not remember where he may have seen her before. She looked so uncomfortable in her heavy wool skirt; so out of place.

Carter was about to ask who she was, but remembered that he wanted to go get some cash out of the bank before it closed, so he tipped his hat towards her and began striding off in the direction of the town's bank.

Kelli watched him for a moment, unsure what to do, but finally determined not to lose this one opportunity, she took a few hurried steps, caught up with the well-built man and began to walk beside him.

"Um, sir, I'm sorry if it was rude of me, but I overheard your conversation in the store just now."

Carter swung his head around and stopped walking. Once again the red rose up in his cheeks, but his eyes sparkled with anger more than embarrassment. "Yes?" His voice rang with indignation. He had been sure that no one else was in the store, so she must have been hiding on purpose to eavesdrop on his conversation.

"Well sir, I was wondering if I might do?"

Carter stared at the girl indignantly, all the while trying to place her and to understand just what she was talking about. "What do you mean?" he finally growled.

Kelli took a breath and let it out to steady her nerves. She looked the young man straight in the eyes and asked, "Will I do for a wife?"

Chapter 2

The blush rose in Kelli's cheeks as the question tumbled out. She could hardly believe she had dared ask him. Silence stretched between them. The man did not respond, but a look of surprise was etched on his face. It took a few seconds for him to regain control of his emotions.

"I don't think we have ever met before." Carter looked at her curiously. He still felt annoyed that she had overheard his conversation about looking for a mail order bride. He had hoped to keep his search for a wife a secret, but now there was no hope.

"No, I just arrived on the train."

Kelli noticed the blank look on the young man's face, so she began to explain.

"You see, I was traveling on the Orphan Train. This was our last stop and tomorrow we will return to New York. I find that I do not want to go back to the city, but the only way that I can keep from returning is to find a job." Carter still looked confused. "Unfortunately, there does not seem to be any jobs in this town for a woman."

"What Orphan Train?" Carter asked, unable to grasp the woman's entire conversation. He did take notice that she was very attractive, even in her dull black skirt and a high collared shirt with small buttons all up the front.

"The Orphan Train out of New York. There is actually only one orphan left at this point though," Kelli answered. She saw the perplexity on Carter's face. "Haven't you ever heard of the Orphan Trains?"

"Yes, but it has never come to this town! I'm on the town council. We have talked about allowing an Orphan Train to come to town, but we have not voted yet."

"This town was on our schedule by mistake. When we arrived, we found no one in town knew we were coming. There must have been some kind of mix up in New York. So, Sister Marter, Charlie and I are staying over night at the hotel. We leave tomorrow. That is why I was at the store.

I was hoping to find work. But as I said, there are no jobs."

The woman's story sounded strange, yet Carter was intrigued.

"So marriage is the next best thing?" Carter asked in amazement. He really could not believe the impudence of the girl, offering to become his wife because she could not find a job in town.

"It seems my only chance." Kelli swallowed, anxious that the man would not accept her offer, yet terrified he would. "You could tell people that I am your mail order bride. I am from New York."

Carter took a closer look at the woman and laughed. "You are not more than a child yourself." She was definitely not the woman he had imagined when he thought about a mail order bride. However, she was rather lovely.

"I am nineteen, sir. I just look young for my age. How old are you? You don't look much older than me." Kelli slapped a hand over her mouth. She could not believe she had just said that to this giant of a man.

"I am twenty three." Carter stood up taller, a stern look crossed his face as if he were trying to make himself seem older.

Kelli observed him closely. As far as she could tell he did not seem to have a flaw of any kind. She stepped back for a moment, wondering if there was something terribly wrong with him. It seemed odd that someone who seemed so perfect would need a stranger for a bride.

A young man, as handsome as Carter, should be able to have any wife he wanted. Kelli bit her bottom lip. "Aren't there any ladies here in town you like?" Kelli asked hesitantly. She realized that she knew nothing about the man, except that he was gorgeous. Even though he had brilliant blue eyes and a smile that made her knees feel weak, she wondered if there were some hidden problem with him.

Carter stared at her for a moment incredulously. He wondered how such a tiny girl could have so much nerve. He could not even believe that he was actually having this conversation with her.

"Not that it is any business of yours, but most of the single women in this town are older than me." Carter's voice began to rise in irritation. He did not feel that he needed to justify his search for a new wife to this tiny slip of a girl.

Suddenly, Carter noticed that several people on the street had stopped and were staring at him and the girl curiously. If they continued their conversation here, there would be no way to stop the town tongues from wagging.

"Would you like to get a lemonade at the hotel with me?"

Kelli smiled. Now she was getting somewhere. "Yes, I would!"

Carter took her hand and slipped it into the crook of his arm. She was sure that Sister Marter would not approve, but she wasn't going to rudely pull away from the man. She had seen other couples strolling in this fashion, so she assumed it was acceptable in public. As she walked beside the handsome man, her heart beat quickly. She felt proud beside him, even though he towered over her.

Carter hurried them quickly up the street, passing the saloon, the barber, the bank, and the small office that housed the local newspaper. He was glad when they finally reached the Emporia Hotel.

As they stepped into the lobby, Kelli's eyes darted around the room, afraid that Sister Marter would be standing there looking for her. When she saw that the room was empty, she relaxed.

The hotel had a small restaurant, where they served meals for the guests. Carter steered Kelli towards it. Once inside, he led her to a table in a private corner. Carter pulled out a chair for her and Kelli gingerly sat.

Carter sat tensely until the waitress had taken the order for two lemonades. He swept the room with a glance. No one else was sitting anywhere near their table. He sat back and relaxed. There was no way anyone from town could overhear their conversation now. He had purposely set himself at the very back of the room, looking out. If anyone he knew entered the room, he would see them before they would even notice him and hopefully he would be able to avoid an embarrassing situation.

Kelli sipped her lemonade enthusiastically. She had never actually had the sweet drink before. It tasted like a little bit of sunshine mixed with sugar. After a few more sips she set her glass down and looked up at Carter.

"So, do you think I will do as a wife for you?" Kelli's words interrupted Carter's thoughts.

"I'm sorry," Carter turned his attention back to the young woman, "have you even told me your name yet?"

"Kelli, and yours is Carter. I overheard the man at the general store call you that. I don't mind using first names if you don't."

"No, I suppose that would be alright," Carter mumbled. He was so disconcerted by the boldness of this young woman, he wasn't really sure what was appropriate or not. "Now, about this marriage business, I think you are too young for what I need."

Kelli almost choked on her next sip of lemonade. "What do you mean, for what you need? I pretty much know what being a wife means, and I think I am able to fulfill the requirements. I can cook, clean, and sew. I'm strong enough to haul water and help with any other chores that you need done. What else do you want?"

"I need a wife who can be a mother." Kelli sat up straighter with interest. She longed to be a mother. She wanted to have a child of her own that no one could ever take away from her.

"A mother? I suppose in time, I would be a mother." Kelli's cheeks turned pink.

"That is exactly what I mean. I can't wait. I need a mother now."

Kelli stared at him perplexed. Gradually a thought occurred to her. "Do you have a child who needs caring for?"

Carter realized that he was not going about this very well. He found talking to a total stranger about getting married very bewildering to him. He was relieved that she seemed to understand what he was talking about, so he decided to just continue to explain the situation the best that he could.

"Yes, I do," Carter began to clarify. "My wife died giving birth, and the baby is only seven months old. I've been struggling to care for her properly and work my farm. I thought that a mail order bride would be the answer, but I haven't had any response to my ad. I guess most women don't want to start off a marriage with someone else's baby."

Kelli nodded her head in understanding and sympathy. She knew all too well how difficult it was for a man to take care of a baby. That was one reason there were so many orphans in New York. Men who had lost their wives, often brought the babies to the orphanage. She also realized that most women, young enough to interest Carter, would not want to get married to a man who already had a child.

"I've hired several different women from town to take care of the baby while I work. Not one of them has been very satisfactory. The women all have homes of their own to care for, so they don't really give her the exclusive care I think she needs. I want someone who is willing to be there all day, every day. I want someone the child can grow up calling mother."

Carter had been looking away as he spoke, but turned back to the young woman.

"I do not personally need a wife and I'm not looking for love. All I need is a mother for my child."

Kelli was about to reply when she noticed a boy's small head pop around the corner, looking in the restaurant. It was Charlie. Kelli wondered what he was doing out of the room without Sister Marter. Although she wanted to continue the discussion with Carter, she knew her first responsibility was to take care of Charlie.

"Excuse me just a minute." Kelli slipped from her chair. She hurried out of the room and quickly found Charlie before he was able to sneak out the front door of the hotel.

"What are you doing down here?" Kelli whispered, in a semi angry tone, to the boy. Charlie knew from past experience that she was irritated at him but she wasn't really angry.

"I wasn't tired, and Sister Marter is snoring," Charlie complained. "I wanted to look around this town. Can't we go out for a walk?" He turned big eyes towards her and a quivering lip.

Kelli's heart melted. She understood his feelings. She too was eager to look around the town more, but she needed to finish her conversation with Carter. That was even more important.

Kelli looked over her shoulder, to see if Carter had followed her, but the lobby was empty. H*e must think I am crazy, running off like I did.*

Kelli reached down and hugged the child. "If you can behave like a gentleman, you can come in to the restaurant here and have a nice glass of lemonade with me."

Charlie's eyes lit up with excitement. He had never tasted lemonade before. In fact, he had never even heard of it, but if Kelli was offering, he knew it would be good.

Charlie eagerly followed Kelli as she walked back to the table and sat down. For just a second the boy hesitated when he saw the large man seated at the table. Kelli smiled reassuringly, so Charlie slipped into the chair, but he eyed the stranger warily.

******

Carter had no idea who this new addition to the table was, but he smiled at the boy. Children were one of Carter's biggest weaknesses. He loved kids. He watched as Kelli handed her glass of lemonade to the boy. Carter grinned as the child took a small sip and then a large gulp. In seconds, the boy was quietly engrossed, enjoying the drink. Carter wondered who the child was, but once Kelli knew that the boy was content she jumped back into the conversation.

"Carter, you surprised me when you told me that you had a baby. Now I understand why you are having trouble getting a wife. I agree with you that not many women want to start off their married life raising someone else's child. But that doesn't matter to me."

Kelli reached over and wiped a drop of lemonade off Charlie's chin. She took these few seconds to prepare the words she wanted to say to the man. When she finally sat back up she turned to Carter and spoke.

"I've worked in an orphanage since I was twelve. I've worked with the infants for seven years so I know that I can raise your baby. I would love to do it."

Carter gave her his full attention nos.

"I love babies more than anything in the world. I've always wanted to be a real mother."

Carter noticed the young boy's head bobbing up and down in agreement.

Kelli noted how Carter kept looking at Charlie. She was pleased that he didn't seem irritated by the boy's presence. She would not want to tie herself to a man who could not be patient with children.

Charlie set the glass down for a moment, but it was very close to the edge of the table. Carter swept his hand out and caught the glass before it tumbled to the ground. Kelli was glad to see that he did not get angry.

Charlie needs a father like him, she thought. Immediately another decision popped into her mind. She sat up and looked Carter straight in the eyes.

"Carter, I'm willing to marry you and raise your baby, but I have one condition," Kelli spoke very seriously. She slipped her hand over one of Charlie's hands. "This is Charlie, he is the last boy left on the Orphan Train. No one wanted to adopt him so far and the trip is over. Now he will have to go back to New York."

Carter glanced at Charlie. Kelli could see the sympathy in his eyes.

"So here is my offer," Kelli continued. "I will marry you and raise your baby as my own. I will be a good mother. I will cook and clean and sew for you as well. If you don't want to love me, that will be alright too. But, I am a package deal. I come with Charlie. I have raised him since he was born and I would not be able to allow him to return to New York without me. In a way, he is my own child."

Kelli knew she was taking a risk by asking this man to include Charlie in the deal, but she hated the idea of sending the boy back to the orphanage without her. She wasn't sure she would even stay behind if Charlie had to go back to New York. She knew that without her, Charlie had little chance of being happy at the orphanage.

"Of course, I would expect you to treat him like your own son," Kelli added.

Charlie had been curiously listening to Kelli and the stranger talking. He understood what the conversation was about. His eyes grew wide in wonder, the glass of sweet drink shook in his hands. Suddenly, he set his glass down and stood up.

"Mister, I think it's great what Kelli is trying to do, but I got to be honest with you," Charlie spoke directly to Carter.

Carter was surprised, but intrigued when the sober look spread across the child's face, making him look much older than he was.

Charlie stepped further away from the table so that Carter could now see the brace on his leg. "There are some things I can't do very well because of my leg, but I'm willing to try really hard. If you take me with Kelli, I'll do the very best I can."

Tears filled Kelli's eyes as she watched the brave boy give his speech. Carter even felt as if he needed to wipe a bit of moisture from his eyes. Carter leaned forward and took the young boy's hand in his.

"I'm sure that you will be able to do just about anything you set your mind to."

Charlie's eyes lit up with pride. Carter ruffled the boy's hair.

"I don't want to seem too pushy," Kelli interrupted, "but this whole thing needs to be settled as soon as possible or Charlie and I will have to leave on the train tomorrow."

Carter sat back and observed Kelli. She was a beautiful young woman, although plainly dressed. She looked nothing like his late wife, but her brown hair glittered with streaks of gold that reminded him of his daughter's hair. He could tell by the way she cuddled Charlie and allowed him to drink her lemonade that she had a heart for children. In fact, he could not imagine finding anyone more qualified to raise his daughter than a person like Kelli who had helped raise children at an orphanage. By the way that Charlie leaned into her, Carter could tell that Kelli had been a great influence on him.

The fact that she wanted him to keep the boy didn't bother him. Carter had always wanted a son and this child, with his wise looking eyes, had already touched his heart.

"What is the meaning of this!" Carter's thoughts were interrupted by a harsh sounding voice. His head swung up. Standing beside the table, was a very severe and angry looking nun.

"Oh dear," Kelli whispered as she stood up.

"I'm waiting for an answer." Sister Marter stared angrily at Kelli. "I have been frantic since I awoke, wondering what had become of you and Charlie. I've walked up and down the boardwalk for the last few minutes hoping to find you in one of the stores. I even braved looking into the sinful saloon, afraid you had wandered in there by mistake."

"I'm sorry, Sister Marter, but the room was so stifling. Charlie and I just wanted to get some air."

Charlie was smart enough not to speak, but his head bobbed up and down in agreement.

"What are you doing here, and with this strange man?" Sister Marter asked, turning her accusing gaze on the man. Carter felt as if he were guilty of a sin worthy of punishment by death.

Kelli opened her mouth to explain, but Carter stopped her, by placing his hand on hers. He stood up so that he could have the advantage over the irate woman.

"Excuse me, Ma'am," his voice drawled, respectfully. "My name is Carter Hardy. I asked Miss Kelli and Charlie to enjoy some lemonade with me. I hope that you will join us as well. We do have something to discuss with you." He pulled out a chair and indicated that she should sit down.

"Me! What could you have to discuss with me?" Sister Marter flushed and stepped back from the powerfully built man. She was upset, but she was also wary of this man. "You are a total stranger to me and I am in charge of these two. Come along Kelli, come along Charlie," she insisted and turned as if to leave.

"Sister Marter, do please join us for a glass of lemonade. There really is something that we need to discuss with you," Kelli pleaded.

Sister Marter was shocked by the tone of Kelli's voice. She had never spoken so boldly before. Sister Marter frowned, expecting them to follow her, but even Charlie who always obeyed, refused to move.

Kelli and Carter sat back down. Sister Marter realized that she had no choice but to join them. She huffed a bit, but finally sat and asked what this was all about. They both refused to discuss anything until she was served a cold glass of lemonade, although she tried to refuse it.

The first sip of lemonade was as heavenly for Sister Marter as it had been for Kelli and Charlie. For just a moment, the harsh look on her face disappeared. Charlie asked if she liked it.

"Yes, it is very good," she set the glass down. "But now, I want to know what is going on here. What are you doing with this man?" She turned to Kelli, ignoring Carter.

Kelli opened her mouth to answer, but Carter reached across the table and covered her hand with his once more. Kelli stopped speaking. Sister Marter's head shot up at the man's boldness. She was about to slap the man's hand away from Kelli's when he shocked her to her core with his words.

"Sister Marter, I would like to adopt Charlie and marry Miss Kelli"

Chapter 3

Kelli almost burst out laughing at the look on Sister Marter's face when Carter made that announcement. First there was shock, then anger, and then indignation.

Sister Marter instantly stood up. "Kelli, Charlie we need to leave right now." The tone of her voice bode no arguing.

"But Sister Marter," Kelli pleaded.

"No Kelli. This is the most ridiculous thing I have ever heard. You do not even know this man. How dare he ask to marry you."

Carter sat looking as innocent as a lamb. Sister Marter nearly snorted in disgust until Kelli spoke up. "But Sister... I asked him."

"You what?"

"I asked him. I overheard a conversation at the general store. He was telling the owner that he wanted a mail order bride. I asked him if I would do."

Sister Marter turned back to the man. She was breathless and distraught. "I cannot even begin to fathom what would have possessed Kelli to do something like this. I do not hold you responsible and I do not expect you to marry the girl just because she asked," Sister Marter assured Carter.

He just continued to smile at her.

Sister Marter continued in a huffy voice. "I also do not believe in men ordering a wife from the city, but that is neither here nor there. I will take Kelli and Charlie back to our room. You needn't worry that she will bother you any longer."

Carter sat patiently while the nun spoke and allowed her to finish, but then he spoke up. "Sister Marter, may I call you that?" Sister Marter nodded slightly. "I'm sure this has all come as quite a surprise to you. Believe me, I am as surprised as anyone, but Kelli is right. I was hoping to hear from an ad that I placed in the city newspaper for a mail order bride. I need a mother to raise my seven month old daughter. Kelli has assured me she can do the job. I am also willing to adopt Charlie as part of the deal."

Charlie interrupted. "Kelli can do it, Sister Marter. She is real good with babies."

"That is beside the point, Charlie." Sister Marter hushed the boy.

"No, that is the point," Kelli argued. "I do not want to return to New York. I do not want to spend my life working in an orphanage. This is my one and only chance to have a home and a family. I want to raise Carter's baby. I want to marry him."

Sister Marter shook her head. "You don't know what you are saying, Kelli. You can't just step into someone else's family and call it your own. What about love?"

Kelli was surprised to hear Sister Marter talk about anything so sentimental. In all the years she had lived in the orphanage, Sister Marter had never shown one ounce of sentimentality. She had often scoffed about romance when the teen girls would ask if they could read a love story.

"Sister, you know that I will never have a chance to find love at the orphanage. I probably won't even have a chance to meet anyone I could ever marry. At least by marrying Carter, I will have Charlie and a baby girl to love."

Carter cleared his throat, feeling embarrassed by the conversation. "I am not promising that I will love Kelli as I loved my wife, but I do promise to take care of her and Charlie. Living on the Kansas Prairie is not an easy life, but I will do all I can to make sure that Kelli and Charlie have everything they could ever need or want. I have a nice home and I've been lucky with my crops for several years. You do not have to worry that I cannot provide a good life for them. I believe that I can offer them a more comfortable life than living at an orphanage."

Sister Marter flashed Carter a look that usually frightened anyone into obeying her, but Carter did not even cringe. Instead, he calmly continued to discuss the marriage plans, as if they were already all settled.

"We can get the judge to perform the ceremony today. He is a circuit judge and won't be back here for several months. If all goes well, I can have Kelli and Charlie settled into their new home by sundown tonight."

"Tonight! That is impossible. Perhaps if Kelli were to stay here, at the hotel for a few weeks and you were to court her properly, she would have the chance to get to know you better. Then in a month, if she still agrees, you can get married. Charlie will have to act as chaperone because I have to return to New York tomorrow." Sister Marter twisted her hands in frustration.

Carter wasn't happy with that plan. He wanted to get back to the farm as quickly as possible. In a few weeks it would be time to begin to harvest the wheat. There was no way he could stay here and court Kelli. He might be able to drive into town on Sundays, but he couldn't spare any more time than that; still, he was sensitive to Sister Marter's thoughts.

"No, Sister Marter," Kelli interjected. "I am ready to marry Carter today! He needs a mother for his little girl right away."

A smile swept over Carter's face. Charlie bounced up and down.

"Please believe me, this is what I really want, Sister," Kelli assured the woman quietly.

Sister Marter sat silently, staring at the glass in her hand. She knew that marriages of convenience were often appropriate in New York, and she had heard that marriages were always swift in the West. She also recognized that Kelli was absolutely right; she would have no chance to ever meet a man and get married while living and working at the orphanage in New York, especially not to such a handsome man.

"...and I think that the fresh air out here will be good for Charlie too," Kelli added softly.

Sister Marter seemed to have run out of arguments. She sighed in resignation. "I don't know how I will explain this to anyone."

"Then, you will allow it?"

"Although it goes against my best judgment, I really cannot stop you. You are old enough to make your own choices now, Kelli."

"What about me?" Charlie asked. Once more his lip quivered slightly.

"Yes, I want to adopt Charlie," Kelli insisted.

Sister Marter sighed. "I think that would be alright. I'm not sure what Father Timothy will say."

Kelli leaned over and hugged Sister Marter. "Please be happy for Charlie and I."

Charlie slipped over and put his arms around the nun's neck. "We are going to be happy here, Sister Marter. We are going to be a real family."

Seeing that Sister Marter had finally given in, Carter stood up. He decided to *'get while the getting was good.'*

"Would you like to walk down to the sheriff's office now?" Carter watched for any hesitation from Kelli, because he really did not want to force her into making this decision too quickly. "I think the judge is there."

"Yes, I'm ready." Kelli took one last sip of the lemonade, placed the glass on the table and stood. "Will you come to the ceremony, Sister?"

Sister Marter reluctantly followed as the others eagerly headed towards the sheriff's office. Charlie slipped between Kelli and Carter. They each took one of his hands in theirs. From behind them, Sister Marter did have to agree that they made a lovely looking family.

Sister Marter did not smile during the entire ceremony and several times she considered interrupting the judge to protest this hasty marriage, but at the very end, when Carter gently kissed Kelli on the cheek, she lifted her hand and wiped a small tear out of the corner of her eye.

Kelli had been the closest thing she ever had to a daughter and she knew that she would miss the girl and Charlie at the orphanage. The only consolation she felt, was knowing that Charlie would grow up in the country, with a father and a mother, rather than live out his life at the orphanage.

Kelli stood beside Carter after the short ceremony. She was tempted to laugh at the absurdity of it all. This wedding had been nothing like the wedding she had always dreamt about.

Instead of the creamy white gown she had always imagined, Kelli wore her plain, serviceable gray dress that the orphanage had given her. There had been no flowers, no veil, no ring, no bridesmaids. There had been only the judge, the sheriff, Sister Marter, Kelli, Carter and Charlie.

When the judge asked them both to sign the marriage certificate, Kelli wondered for a split moment if she had done the right thing. She sent up a silent prayer, *Lord, have I made the right decision for Charlie and for me?* But then she noted Carter standing beside Charlie with his hand gently tossed on top of the boy's head. It was obvious that Carter liked Charlie and she could see that Charlie already adored the man. That alone was worth giving up any daydreams she ever had. Kelli stepped forward contently and signed the paper.

The sheriff pounded Carter on the back with congratulations and the judge shook his hand. They both insisted on giving the bride a kiss. Each placed a brotherly kiss on her cheek. Sister Marter obviously did not approve, but stuttered in embarrassment when the men stepped up on either side of her and placed a brotherly kiss on her cheeks as well.

******

Carter, Kelli, Charlie and Sister Marter stepped out of the sheriff's office. The sun blinded them for a second. Kelli's eyes roamed up and down the street, taking in her new hometown.

"Would you like to do some shopping?" Carter whispered into Kelli's ear. His breath was warm and sent a pleasant shiver down her spine.

"Shopping? For what?"

"For whatever you and Charlie will need." Carter steered her towards the general store while Kelli wondered what Carter thought they needed. She had two dresses and Charlie had a small suitcase with his clothes from the orphanage. He was wearing the nice suit they had supplied for his trip on the Orphan Train. Aside from that, they both owned night clothes as well. Nothing was new or fancy, but Kelli couldn't think what more they needed.

On their way to the store, Sister Marter insisted that she needed to return to the hotel. The excitement had been hard on her and she needed to rest before the long journey back to New York the next day. Once again, Kelli hugged the woman, and then Charlie took his turn. To Sister Marter's amazement, Carter stepped up and gave her a hug as well.

"I promise to take care of them." Carter assured her.

"Can we meet for dinner?" Sister Marter asked. Kelli turned hopeful eyes to Carter, but he shook his head.

"It will take a while to get back to the farm. If we wait until after dinner, it will be too dark."

"I see." Sister Marter nodded in understanding. "Then I suppose I should say good-bye now." Kelli and Charlie both hugged Sister Marter again. Kelli thanked her several times for allowing them to adopt Charlie.

"Promise to write and tell me all about your new life," Sister Marter whispered into Charlie's ear.

"I promise." Charlie's eyes held back tears.

As Sister Marter walked towards the hotel alone, Charlie squeezed Kelli's hand.

"I think she's happy for us, even if she seems angry."

Kelli hugged the boy close to her. "I know she is."

Carter encouraged his new family to move on towards the general store. When they entered, Carter led them straight up to the counter. The old Welsh man looked up in surprise at the three of them, standing in front of the counter, smiling at him.

"Just wanted to introduce you to my wife and son," Carter's voice boomed through the store. The older man's face registered shock. "This is Kelli and Charlie."

Kelli's face flushed when she noticed the man barely acknowledged her. He just turned to Carter and spoke. "Well, Mr. Hardy, I'm plain out surprised. I still don't see what was wrong with one of the women in this town. There were plenty of them here for you to choose a wife from. Don't know why you had to hook up with an orphan."

For a moment, Carter actually looked like he had been struck. It never dawned on him that the people of the town would care one way or another who he married, but he quickly recovered. No matter what people thought, he was not going allow anyone to be rude to his family.

Carter stepped towards the counter and leaned as close to the man as he could. "As I was saying. This is my wife and my son now. They are not orphans. They are my family, and I hope you will treat them with the same respect you have always shown me."

Kelli saw the man take several gulps. She could tell that he realized he had made a mistake. Kelli almost laughed when she saw how quickly he changed his tune. "Of course, Carter. Glad to meet you, Mrs. Hardy. Can I help you find anything today?"

Kelli hid a secret smile behind her hand. It didn't matter to her what the people of the town thought about her. She had been called many bad names in her lifetime. But it was nice to have someone stand up for her.

"Okay, Kelli, you go ahead and shop. I'll just show Charlie around a bit," Carter insisted. He and Charlie turned away.

Kelli wandered around the store, but really had no idea what to select. She had never been shopping as an adult, because that had not been her job in the orphanage. For once in her life, Kelli wished that Sister Marter were here. Kelli had no idea where to begin. She could not even begin to imagine what exactly Carter thought she and Charlie would need.

As Kelli meandered, Carter showed Charlie around the store, but soon realized that Kelli had not made any selections. When he stepped over to ask her why, he noted the tears in her eyes. Carter took her hands in his.

"What's wrong Kelli?" he whispered, a slight worried look on his brow.

"I've never had to shop before." Kelli spoke softly so that the store owner would not hear her. "At the orphanage they had someone else do all the shopping. I don't have any idea what Charlie and I will need. We both have enough already I think."

Carter felt a sting of pity shoot through his heart.

"What do you have with you?"

Kelli told him. Carter listened, but shook his head. "You will need more than that. Don't worry, we can shop together this time. If you are like most women, it won't be long before you have the hang of it."

Kelli wondered what he meant, but gratefully fell in beside him. Carter gathered things up and place them on the counter. Kelli wondered what many of them were for. Some of the personal items that Carter picked made Kelli blush, especially the undergarments, but she was thrilled to think that she would own such wonderful things.

At one point, Carter picked Charlie up, sat him on the counter and asked the store owner to find some good sturdy work boots for him. The owner noted the brace on Charlie's leg and smirked, but when he saw the stern look flash across Carter's face he rushed away and brought out a pair of sturdy boots that were large enough around to cover part of the brace on the boy's leg.

Charlie's eyes lit up. "For me? Really!"

"Yes, Son. Every man needs a good pair of boots." Charlie's smile grew wider. He slipped the boots on and hopped down from the counter happily. Then Carter turned back to Kelli.

"You did say you can sew? If we pick material out, can you make clothes for you and the boy?"

Kelli nodded. She had sewn most of the children's clothing at the orphanage, but the pile on the counter was already so overwhelming. She couldn't see how Carter could afford to pay for material as well. It never occurred to Kelli that marrying her would cost the man so much.

"We can get by with what we have," Kelli spoke in a hushed tone.

Carter eyed her dress. "You won't be able to work very well in that dress."

Kelly blushed.

"You need several lighter calicoes," Carter insisted. "And Charlie can't very well milk a cow wearing that Sunday get up he has on."

"Am I gonna milk a cow?" Charlie nearly shouted.

"Sure you are!" Carter patted him and pulled a candy stick out of one of the jars on the counter. He handed it to Charlie. Charlie stared at the candy in amazement then looked at Kelli for permission to eat it. Kelli nodded and Charlie slipped the candy stick into his mouth. Kelli giggled at the look of joy on the boy's face.

Carter reached back into the jar, selected several more pieces of candy and put them in a small bag. He added the bag to the pile. Charlie didn't even dare to hope that the candy was for him.

When the store owner announced the total that Carter owed, Kelli swallowed hard. Her hands were sweating. She was sure that Carter was going to be angry about the cost, but instead he pulled out some money, tossed it on the counter, flashing a sly grin at Kelli.

"How did you like your first shopping spree?" He laughed. Kelli looked up at him nervously. She could see the merriment in his eyes and she felt a bit of relief.

"It's a lot of money. Are you sure we need it all?"

"Sure, I'm sure. In a week or two, we can come back to get everything we forgot. We might even have to look through the Montgomery Wards Catalog."

Carter lifted one bag and walked out the door. Kelli stood stock still wondering what else she could ever need, and then she wondered what a Montgomery Wards Catalog was.

At the door, Carter turned back and shook his head in amazement. The two misfits, that he had just made his family, gathered up the rest of the packages and walked towards him. For a moment he wondered if he had gone crazy.

But when Charlie stomped up beside him and said, "Thanks for the boots, Pa." Carter was sure that he had done the right thing.

Kelli overheard Charlie call Carter 'Pa'. She glanced over at her new husband to see if he minded. From the smile on his face, Kelli could tell that Carter did not seem to mind at all.

"You coming with us?" Carter called back over his shoulder to Kelli as he and Charlie carried their packages out to the buckboard wagon.

Kelli looked up at Carter and nodded.

"Then grab some of those packages and let's get going home."

It had been the most unusual and exciting day of her life, and Kelli couldn't help feeling a warmth spread through her soul.

"Thank-you, Lord," Kelli whispered towards heaven, "for giving me a home! A home of my own."

Chapter 4

Charlie and Kelli gladly helped carry the packages out and placed them into Carter's wagon, but once more before they left, Kelli tried to approach him about returning some of the items. The price he had paid was more money than Kelli would have earned in years working at the orphanage. She did not realize how much it would cost for Carter to take on two more family members.

"Please Kelli, don't fuss. I am a fairly wealthy man and this little bit of money won't put me in the poorhouse," Carter reassured her. "Besides, being married is going to save me a lot of money."

"Why is that?"

"Now I don't have to pay people to watch the baby." Carter headed back into the store to get the last package.

Kelli stood stock still for a moment. She had forgotten about the baby. That was why Carter married her in the first place. She needed to remember that. He wanted a mother for his child, not a wife to love. When he spoke the words out loud though, it felt like a slap in her face.

As Kelli watched the tall, handsome man she would now call husband, loading the last packages onto the wagon, a small ache filled her heart. She had to admit to herself that she did want to be loved, and although she would have a life outside of the orphanage and be able to raise Charlie as her own, she would now never have the chance to find a man who would love her, cherish her and treat her like a real wife.

Kelli's heart twisted as she reminded herself that this new life was just another job; a more pleasant job than the one at the orphanage, but still only a job. She must not forget again.

Please Lord, help me to be content in this new life! Kelli prayed.

Carter had been watching Kelli from the corner of his eye as he loaded the wagon. He noticed how she seemed to freeze up when he mentioned the baby and it confused him. When he had first told her about the child she had seemed so eager to get married and be a mother. Now he wondered if she really wanted to be a mother after all.

Carter began to worry that perhaps Kelli really only wanted to get married so that she wouldn't have to return to the orphanage. Maybe she had lied about loving children. His stomach ached just thinking about it.

What have I done? Oh Lord, what have I done? His soul groaned.

"Are we ready to go to our new home now?" Charlie's happy words broke the spell of doubt that had enveloped both Carter and Kelli. At the same time, they both looked up at one another across the wagon, with unanswered questions in their eyes.

Carter walked back around and helped Kelli onto the wagon, then he swung Charlie up into the buckboard. Charlie happily settled down in the back, with his feet dangling over the edge. Kelli tried to get comfortable on the hard buckboard seat, but it wasn't much better than the rigid seats in the train.

Carter finally jumped up onto the seat beside her, grabbed the reins, gave a small crack on the two horses' backs. The horses began walking slowly down the dirt street, heading away from town.

"Here we go, Kelli, off to our new home!" Charlie shouted. Kelli's heart squeezed with concern.

Have I done the right thing?

As the horses made their way down the main street of Emporia, which was named 'Merchant Street', Kelli and Charlie gazed at the buildings that lined the street. There was a shoe store, a harness shop, a clothing store, a pharmacy and several other businesses besides the general store and the hotel.

Carter turned the horses towards the end of the main road, and then steered the beasts onto a well-worn dirt road that headed away from town. As far as Kelli could see, there was not a building or house in sight.

More worries filled her mind. She wondered how often they would come to town. Carter said they could return soon, to buy more items if they needed, but other than that, she wondered if he had any other reason for leaving his farm. She wondered what a life, far away from people, would be like.

A small tinge of fear crept into her soul. *What if I hate living in the country, on a farm?* Kelli squeezed her eyes shut to keep back the tears that threatened to start flowing. *What if Carter is cruel to Charlie? How will I get him away if we live so far away from town?*

Kelli kept lifting up prayers to ease her anxiety. After a short time she began to feel better, as God soothed her. She was hopeful that the peace she felt was an indication that this was the plan God had for her life.

As the horses plodded along, Kelli watched Carter handle them. She had seen horses in New York but had never been so close to them before. She was intrigued by the way they swished their tails back and forth as they walked. The horses seemed eager to trudge along without much assistance from Carter. Kelli assumed they were happy to be on their way home.

Carter noticed Kelli's interest in the horses. "If you want to learn to drive the team, I will teach you. That way you can come to town if you need to, whenever I am busy."

Kelli was amazed. It seemed as if Carter was reading her mind. She gulped. Just looking at the horses was frightening; she could not imagine actually being able to drive them, but it would be a good thing to know how. She didn't think that she would ever willingly go to town alone, however.

"I would like that," she murmured in a noncommittal voice.

Carter nodded, struck again by how different she seemed. They rode along in silence for a time. Kelli thought more about the new life she had agreed to. She wondered if it really mattered if Carter loved her. She had been looking for any kind of job to keep from returning to the orphanage; this marriage just happened to fulfill the need. She loved children and she knew that she could do a good job raising his baby. She had only started thinking about love when she had first gazed into Carter's steady face.

Was he a man she could love? She had never even considered that love would come into her life before. Life in the orphanage had not encouraged her to hope.

The wagon swayed suddenly. Kelli sat up straight and grabbed on to the side. Carter flashed her an apologetic grin. She shook her head and reminded herself that he had made it clear that he was not interested in love. He wanted a mother for his baby.

"What is the baby's name?" Kelli asked. She determined to get her fanciful thoughts under control and to begin her job correctly.

Carter started when Kelli's voice broke the silence between them.

"Her name is Susan."

"That is a lovely name."

"Her mother thought so." Carter turned his eyes away. Kelli could feel the presence of sadness surrounding him. She felt him withdraw from her. It suddenly dawned on her that he was still suffering from the loss of his wife.

Carter had mentioned that his wife passed away only seven months ago. She knew what that kind of grief felt like, since she had experienced losing her parents. Kelli felt a tightening in her chest; sorrow for Carter's pain engulfed her. She wanted to reach out and hug him, to tell him that everything would be okay, as she had done for the orphans so often, but in this instance Kelli wasn't sure it would be appropriate. She didn't even know if she should pat his hand. Carter was, after all, a grown man. Kelli suspected that he was also still a small boy in some ways.

Sister Marter had once told her that boys never completely grow up, that there is always a part of them that is young, and that no matter how grown up they act, they still need to be reassured. Kelli wanted to give this comfort to Carter, but she felt that their relationship was too new. Instead of reaching out as she longed to do, Kelli turned and watched the scenery pass, giving him time to mourn.

******

Charlie enjoyed riding on the end of the buckboard wagon. His legs hung off the back, swaying with the motion of the wagon. He held a hand above his eyes to block out the sunlight as he scanned the horizon.

Charlie didn't want to miss any of the scenery from town, to his new home, three miles south of Emporia. Even though most of the countryside was the same flat plains, with waving fields of grass, there were many things that Charlie had never seen before.

Carter was pulled out of his reverie when Charlie started pointing at different birds and small creatures he saw hiding in the tall grass and calling out, "What's that Pa? What's that?"

Carter was soon busy pointing out several types of birds for Charlie. "There's a Western Meadow Lark." It was a yellow, black, and white bird. Carter explained that the bird made its nest on the ground, in the open country. Charlie was intrigued. He only knew about birds that made their nests in trees, and even those, he had never seen up close. Most of the animals he knew anything about, he had only seen in books.

Carter told Charlie about prairie chickens, snipes and geese. The young boy bounced up and down in excitement whenever he noticed something moving in the tall grass, and Carter never seemed to grow tired of answering Charlie's call of, "What's that, Pa?"

Kelli had seen homesteads closer to town, but as the horses plodded further along the dirt road bordered with the high Prairie grass, there were fewer homes. When she did see one, off in the distance, it looked lonely. Kelli wondered if there would be any neighbors near Carter's home.

Charlie did not seem to notice the lack of houses. He was excited with the wide open plains. He had already decided that Carter and Kelli were all the family that he would ever need. Of course, there was the baby as well.

Charlie was used to babies. Because of his leg, there were many times that he stayed behind at the orphanage when the other children went outside to play. He always helped Kelli care for the babies. Over the years he had tried not to get attached to any of them because most of the babies got adopted quickly. He learned that if he cared too much, it hurt when the babies were adopted.

Charlie was secretly excited about this baby, because he would be able to help take care of this one and nobody would be able to take it away.

Kelli sat on the bumpy seat, quietly listening as Carter called out bits of information about birds and other things to Charlie. She was just as interested as Charlie was about it all. When Charlie grew quiet, Kelli turned and looked at the young boy. She smiled. She could tell that he was completely blissful with his new life. She wondered what it would feel like to be able to adjust to change so easily.

Here she was, no longer an orphan, but a married woman, with two children of her own to raise and a husband. Adjusting to all of that in one day was going to be difficult. She wasn't worried about raising the children, or cooking, cleaning, or sewing. She wasn't even concerned about the many new things she would have to learn while living on the Kansas prairie, instead of in a city orphanage. What did worry her though, was adjusting to being a married woman; especially a married woman whose husband was still in love with his first wife.

Kelli's eyes shifted to the man next to her. She was not sitting very close to him. Not the way a real bride would sit next to her brand new husband. Kelli decided, right then and there, not to dwell on these thoughts.

She was just happy that her empty life at the orphanage was over and that she would be with Charlie from now on. Kelli swiped the strands of hair that had slipped out of her braid back into place, sat up straight, and set her eyes forward. She was determined to make this marriage work so that Carter would have no regrets. She would just have to adjust, no matter what this new life held in store for her. It had to be better than the life than she would have lived if she had returned to the New York orphanage.

"Kelli, you know what I think?" Charlie called up over his shoulder.

"No, what do you think!" Kelly laughed.

"I think that God is here with us right now. I can feel Him all around us, can't you?"

Kelli took a deep breath of fresh air and gazed around at the wild plains. "Yes, Charlie. I do think He is here with us."

Kelli glanced at Carter again. He did not seem to notice her comments about God. It suddenly struck her that she really had no idea if Carter was a Christian or not. Dread filled her spirit. Had she been too hasty? She knew that marrying someone who did not share her faith was wrong. She had been taught that she should never be unequally yoked with anyone.

It surprised her that even Sister Marter had not inquired about Carter's beliefs, but, everything had happened so fast.

Kelli shrugged. *I'll just have to believe that God has me where He wants me.* There was little else she could do about it at this point except to pray silently and earnestly for her future.

*****

After traveling for some time, Carter realized that he had been ignoring Kelli. He knew that his behavior wasn't fair to her. She was his wife now, even if in name only. But whenever he tried to speak to Kelli, thoughts of his first wife filled his mind. He could not stop remembering his short marriage. For a moment, he wondered if the pain he felt would ever end.

From the corner of his eye, Carter noted that Kelli had her eyes closed and seemed to be nodding off. It had been a long ride so far and he hadn't made it very pleasant for her. Although he felt saddened about his first wife, it wasn't right to continue to grieve. Life had to go on. He had baby Susan to think about, and now, he had a new wife and a new son.

Carter grinned to himself. "That was quite a trip to town!"

His voice startled Kelli. She jumped and swung her head up to find Carter staring at her. He no longer seemed sad. In fact, now he looked as though he were enjoying his own private joke.

"I'm sorry, what were you saying?"

"Oh, nothing. I'm sorry I've been so quiet."

"That is fine, I understand," Kelli assured him. Carter hated sympathy, but the gentle look on her face comforted him.

"We are almost there. As a matter of fact, we are on my land now." Carter made a sweeping gesture with his hand.

Kelli scanned the horizon. All she could see were more rolling acres of tall Prairie grass. She squinted her eyes, looked in every direction, but saw nothing that appeared to be a homestead. Another wave of insecurity swept over her.

"Where is your house?" her voice squeaked.

"It's over the hill, there." Carter pointed towards the east. Kelli still could not make out anything that even resembled a small house.

"This field is all wheat," Carter explained. "It will be ready to harvest in a month. That is, if it ever rains again."

Worry lines etched themselves across her forehead. Kelli could not help but feel concerned. Carter claimed to be a wealthy man, but was he? Would there be a house anywhere that would be habitable for her and Charlie? She really knew nothing about this man at all. The sheriff in town seemed to like him, but that wasn't enough to base trust on.

I have to trust God, she kept telling herself. *God has a special plan for me, and He led me here.*

"Does it rain here very often?" Kelli placed her hand above her eyes so she did not have to squint, still searching the distance for a building.

"Sure, we had plenty of rain in the spring and early summer, but there has been a real heat wave going on lately. If anything else goes wrong, I will lose this crop."

"What would happen then? Could you lose the land? Could you lose your home?" Her worry frown deepened. Kelli had never considered that life on the prairie might not be as secure as she hoped.

"No need to be concerned about that." Carter patted Kelli's hand when he noticed the frown on her brow. "The land is all paid for, and I have plenty of savings. This is also the last year I plan to grow this kind of wheat. I would hate to lose it, but we would survive. Next year, I plan to grow Turkey Red Wheat. I'll plant it in the fall and harvest it in the spring, before the hot summer months burn it up."

Kelli noticed the look of pride in Carter's eyes. Not arrogance, just pride in the land. Kelli knew little about wheat or harvest, but she smiled and listened. She hoped to become the kind of wife that Carter would feel he could call 'friend', even if that was the closest they could ever be. She was also very interested in everything about her new life.

Carter paused, "I'm sorry, I hate to bore you with the details of farming." Suddenly Carter noticed that during their conversation he had allowed the horses to almost come to a full stop. He clicked the reins and they started moving again quickly. They were anxious to get back to their warm stall.

"Please go on. I'm very interested," Kelli assured him. "If I am going to live on this land, I want to know all about it."

Carter smiled, and a pleasant feeling spread through him. His first wife had never cared about the land. They rarely ever talked about the farm or the wheat. It had never bothered him, but there were times it would have been nice to talk to her about the things he spent his day working on. Carter looked at Kelli again and could tell that she really did seem fascinated, so he continued speaking.

"A few years back, many Mennonite families from Russia moved into this area. They brought the Turkey Red Wheat with them. Most of the farmers around here didn't want to switch, but once I saw how much easier it was to grow, I decided to switch. It's almost time to harvest this wheat, but I'm more excited about next year. I've had a few good years, so I was able to buy the wheat seed for next year ahead of time."

Charlie overheard the conversation and called up to Carter, "Will I be able to help you harvest the wheat?"

Carter remembered the brace on Charlie's leg. "Actually, there will be a lot of work involved and there will be lots of jobs to go around." Carter snuck a peek at Kelli to see her expression about his answer. She smiled and nodded her head in agreement.

"I'm sure there will be enough work for all three of us," Carter added.

Kelli's eyes lit up with eager anticipation. She was never one to shun hard work, and it made her happy to hear Carter talk about including her. She was determined to find out all she could about farming

"Once we harvest the wheat, we take it to Soden's Mill to sell. They grind it down to make flour."

"Really, and then what happens to it?"

"They sell it under the name of 'Four Roses'."

"That is a strange name. I would think they would call it 'Blue Grass Flour'."

Carter chuckled, looking around at the fields of swaying Prairie blue stem grass, "I agree with you." Carter was enjoying the conversation with Kelli. He hoped this meant that they would be able to become good friends in the future. He imagined that living with a woman you couldn't talk to, would not be a very pleasant life.

"It's really beautiful here. Is your land still part of the town of Emporia?"

"Yes, Emporia reaches from the Neosho River, north of town, to the Cottonwood River, south of my land." Kelli had never looked at a map of this area, so she really had no idea what Carter meant, but she was glad to have him talking to her.

"Have you always lived here?"

"No, I grew up on a farm in Ohio."

"You've always been a farmer?"

"My parents raised corn. I had an older brother named Samuel. He served in the Civil War. I was too young to join. I stayed behind and learned to run the farm. When the war ended, I was about thirteen, but my brother never came home." Carter's voice grew soft with the sad memories.

"Oh, I'm sorry." Kelli touched his arm gently. This man had endured so much sorrow in his life already. The one thing that Kelli understood was sorrow.

Carter was surprised at the heat that shot up his arm where Kelli touched him. "It was a long time ago, but when they realized Samuel was not going to come home, my parents decided to move to town. My father was a better blacksmith than farmer. They were happier in town."

"But you weren't?"

"No. I loved farming and missed it. When I was seventeen, I heard that a man could buy six hundred and forty acres of land in Kansas for one dollar an acre. I was so excited about the opportunity. I took my small savings and put it together with money that my parents gave me and came to Kansas on a wagon train. That is where I met my wife Abby. Her family was heading west. We fell in love, got married, and came to Kansas to claim our land. By then I was nineteen years old, and knew more about farming than most of the others who settled in this area. I was able to thrive, while many of my distant neighbors lost their farms and had to move back east or head further west."

Kelli could see sadness slip into Carter's eyes again. "Tell us more about your land," she urged to take his mind off of the memories.

Carter pointed in one direction. "We have a nice creek with plenty of water. It helps when there hasn't been rain for a while. I even catch a fish in it, from time to time."

Charlie's head popped up when he heard the word fish. Before he could ask, Carter answered, "Yes Charlie, you will be able to go fishing with me."

As the wagon drew closer to the top of the hill, Kelli's heart began to pound. What would the house be like? She felt so nervous. When they reached the top, Kelli was confused, she still could see no house. Her heart plummeted.

"Where is the house?" she bravely asked.

"Right under us?" Carter laughed.

Carter headed the wagon down the hill and then turned it around to face the hill. Kelli was intrigued to see that the house was indeed there. It looked as if Carter had built it right up against the hill. It was a lovely wooden house.

"When I first moved here, I lived in a Soddy."

"What's a Soddy?" Charlie quipped.

Kelli was fascinated. "Yes, Carter, tell us more."

Carter was pleased that Kelli was so interested. "A Soddy is a house built out of strips of dried grass and dirt. I thought it would be easier to just dig out a house in the side of a hill for three sides, that way I only had to cut strips for the front. It was plenty big and cozy for a year, but it wasn't long before I was able to build a real house out of wood. I hated to build the house anywhere but here, hidden by this hill, so I just attached the house to the front of the Soddy.

"You mean, you just dug a house out of the side of a hill?" Kelli was amazed.

"Yes. I use the Soddy for storage at the back of the house. Right now I use another old Soddy as a barn. It's behind that hill." Kelli's eyes followed where Carter pointed.

"Can I see the cow?" Charlie interrupted. He had crawled towards the front of the wagon and was bouncing excitedly up and down on the buckboard behind them.

Carter hopped out of the wagon, put his arms out and swung Charlie down to the ground. "Pretty soon, Son. Let's get Kelli settled in the house first." Carter walked around the wagon and reached out to help Kelli down. When she stood, her dress got stuck under her foot. She stumbled forward, falling straight into Carter's arms. Another surge of electricity shot through him, as he held her for a moment; a little longer than necessary.

When he finally set her on the ground, Kelli was blushing. "I'm sorry for being so clumsy." She quickly turned so he would not notice her blushes. Being in Carter's arms had caused a warmth to spread throughout her whole body. It was a wonderful feeling.

"Don't worry about it," Carter mumbled, unable to shake off the jolt he had felt. "I suggest we all go in the house and get settled. Don't expect much."

"I will love it. Remember, I've never had a home."

Carter tried to imagine how Kelli must have felt being an orphan. He was a sensitive man and his heart ached for her, but he wondered if he would ever be able to think of this house as anything but the house he built for Abby, even if Abby had never really been happy with it.

Kelli coughed slightly, pulling Carter's attention back. The anticipation and anxiety on her face as she stood silently staring at the closed front door, reflected his own feelings. He had wanted Abby to love the house he had built for her, but she had not. All she ever wanted was to go back east. As his wife, Carter hoped that Kelli would like the house.

Carter finally pushed open the door, took a deep breath and let it out. "Welcome home Kelli!"

Chapter 5

The house was more amazing than anything Kelli could have imagined. The front door opened into a large, open room. On one end there was a fireplace, with two chairs set in front and a lovely handmade rug on the floor. Next to the fireplace, was an opening that led to a hallway. On the other end of the big room, there was a large wooden table and four chairs. There was an opening on that end, that led into another room. Kelli walked around, gently touching beautiful things that were scattered around. She realized that most of the decorative items must have been made by Carter's first wife, Abby.

Carter watched Kelli move around the room. "Most of the frills were Abby's. She brought them with her."

"They are beautiful. I will be extra careful with them."

"Kelli, this is your house now. If there is anything here you do not want, you can box them up. We can give them to Susan as part of her hope chest someday."

"I'm sure that I will love them. We didn't have things like this in the orphanage."

Carter nodded. "I just want you to know that you can change anything you like."

"I think Susan should grow up with her mother's lovely things around her. If it does not bother you, I would like to keep them out. I've never seen such beautiful items before. I will feel like a princess with such lovely things around."

Carter's eyes swept the room. There was nothing that actually caused sad memories. Abby had very good taste and the items enhanced the otherwise, rough room.

He had no special attachment to the things. He reached out and placed his hands on Kelli's shoulders.

"These things won't bother me, and if you like them, leave them out. Just remember that you are welcome to decorate the house however you see fit. It is your home now."

A small tremor made its way down Kelli's spine from the gentle squeeze that Carter gave her shoulder. She stared into his eyes and for a second got lost in them.

"Thank-you," she whispered and swept her eyes around the room. There was little she would change, but at least now she knew that if she wanted to she could; perhaps add small things to make it more her own.

Just then Charlie tugged on Kelli's hand. So far he had stood quietly, rather awed by the large room.

"This is real pretty, Kelli. Can I sleep by the fire?"

Carter overheard the boy. "Don't you want to sleep in your own room, in a bed?"

Charlie turned around. "I don't see a bed, but I think sleeping in front of that nice fireplace would be great. I won't be cold like I was at the orphanage."

Carter squatted down in front of Charlie. Kelli could see that he was holding his emotions in check. She was about to say something to lighten the moment because she didn't want Carter to feel pity for them, but then Carter pulled Charlie close and gave him a quick hug.

"Son, I promise that you will never be cold again." Carter's voice was husky. "We have lots of blankets and I think that you will enjoy sleeping in a bed."

Charlie eyed the fireplace skeptically. It was hard for him to imagine anything as warm as that, but he was willing to believe what Carter said, so he just nodded his head in agreement.

"Across the room there, is the hallway that leads to the bedrooms." Carter pointed his hand in the general direction. Kelli and Charlie turned their heads to look towards the hallway.

"There are three rooms. They are small but comfortable. Kelli, I think for now you should take the one with the baby. Charlie can have one and I will have one."

Kelli's head whipped around in amazement. She could not believe that he was suggesting separate rooms since they were married. Kelli stared at Carter, the shock in her eyes showing, but he said nothing.

Kelli wanted to speak up and tell Carter that she had hoped to be a real wife to him, but she was too embarrassed. It was obvious now that Carter truly had only wanted a mother for his baby, and not a wife. Her shoulders sank, but she nodded.

Kelli felt somewhat relieved, and a bit disappointed at the same time. She had little idea what being a wife meant even though Sister Marter had pulled her aside and quickly explained a bit about the intimacy between a man and woman. The information had seemed so strange to her and she wasn't sure that she was ready to have that kind of physical relationship with a total stranger, even if he was a gorgeous golden cowboy. But, now it seemed that Carter was not going to even try to have that kind of marriage.

While Kelli stood contemplating her new marriage, and the sleeping arrangements, Charlie jumped up.

"Where is my room?" Charlie yelled and rushed into the hallway. "Come on, Pa, show me which room is mine!" The boy's voice became muffled as he made his way down the hallway.

Carter laughed at the boy's excitement, then turned back to Kelli. "I'll show you your room as well," he said and held out his hand to her.

Kelli stared at Carter's hand for a moment, then reached out and slipped her tiny hand into his large one. They walked across the room and into the hallway together. Since the short marriage ceremony, Carter had treated her very gently. She thought that moments like these were an indication that Carter considered her his real wife, but now she wondered.

"Is this one mine?" Charlie shouted to Carter from the far end of the hallway. "That first one has a big bed, so I thought it was yours, and the next one has a baby bed, but this one has a nice little bed, just my size."

"Yes sir, Buddy, that is your room. Kelli will be in the room next to yours, so she will be close to you if you need her," Carter explained, as they stepped up to the door of the room with the small cradle in it.

Charlie waved his hand, beckoning Kelli to move farther along the hallway.

"Look, Kelli, I get this whole room."

Carter squeezed Kelli's hand. She saw his eyes filled with merriment.

They moved towards the end of the hallway and stepped into the smallest room. Charlie was standing beside the bed. Carter dropped Kelli's hand and moved towards the boy.

"I thought you wanted to sleep by the fire?" Carter ruffled the boy's hair.

Charlie stood still for a moment, staring at Carter, trying to decide if he was joking or not. Once he realized that Carter was only having a bit of fun, Charlie smiled. "Oh, I guess I can try out the bed first."

Kelli looked around. It was small, but very cozy. There was a single bed and a small dresser in the room. Since Charlie had never slept anywhere but at the orphanage, on a small cot, in a room with no less than twenty other boys, she could only imagine that this room looked like a mansion to him. In fact, when she had peeked into the room she would be staying in, she had been pleasantly surprised at how inviting it looked.

"It's a wonderful room," Kelli assured the boy. "Why don't you lay down and rest for a while?"

"I'm not tired," Charlie said emphatically.

"I think we are all tired. It has been a long, exciting day. A little rest will do you good."

Charlie frowned. "I want to see the cow," he whined.

"There will be plenty of time for that." Carter stepped over, scooped the boy up and plopped him playfully on the bed. "I think a short rest would be a good idea. Do you think that this comforter can keep you warm enough?"

"I guess," he mumbled. Charlie was not convinced that he needed a rest, but reluctantly lay back. Carter left the two of them. Kelli pulled the comforter up to Charlie's neck and then sat on the foot of the bed. She sang a few songs that were familiar to the boy. As she had expected, it only took a few minutes for Charlie to fall fast asleep.

When she was sure that Charlie was asleep, Kelli kissed the child's forehead and then made her way out of the room. She wandered down the hallway, peeked into the room where she would be sleeping, and sighed with contentment. The room was just a bit larger than Charlie's room. There was a single bed and a cradle in the room. At the foot of the bed was a hand-carved box. The bed was covered by a lovely quilt.

Kelli stepped into the room and gingerly sat down on the end of the bed. A tear of joy slipped down her cheek. She now had everything she had ever hoped for in life; a home and a family which included Charlie. There was nothing else she could imagine wanting, except to have Carter actually love her.

How can I be so selfish after all God has given me? Kelli reprimanded herself. *I just need to be thankful for everything I do have. I can't expect Carter to love me yet,* she thought. *He doesn't even know me.* Kelli hoped that in time, Carter would come to know her better, and fall in love with her. *Then he may want me as a real wife.*

Kelli crossed her hands and bowed her head.

Thank-you Lord, for this beautiful home. Lord, if it is in your plan, please help me to become the type of woman that Carter will love. Help me to become a real wife to him.

While she sat quietly in prayer, Kelli heard some shuffling noises coming from somewhere in the house. She stood up, smoothed her skirt, and headed out into the hallway again. When she reached the large front room, she saw that Carter had been busy bringing in all the supplies from the wagon.

Carter looked at her, his brow furrowed. He straightened up and stood in the open doorway, holding a box.

"I'm sorry if I disturbed you. I thought you might like a rest too?"

"I think I am too excited to sleep. Everything is so new and amazing. It will take me some time to get adjusted to it all. I was wondering though, when will I get to meet the baby?"

*****

Carter smiled at Kelli. He liked the way her eyes lit up when she spoke. Her enthusiasm for everything new was infectious. It was wonderful to see that she was excited about meeting Susan.

There were many women in town who had been willing to help with Susan, but Carter never felt that any of them really wanted to become a mother to his daughter. Several of them hinted, quite openly, that they wouldn't mind becoming his wife, but Carter wanted someone who would adore Susan.

For a second he considered Kelli. Would she really love Susan? Could he trust this virtual stranger with his daughter? Then he remembered the way she behaved with Charlie. Surely if she treated Charlie so well, she would be good to Susan.

"My neighbor has Susan. I will ride over tonight and pick her up." Carter did not want to go into any details about the woman who was currently watching Susan. She was the worst of the bunch. She was always hinting, hoping that Carter would marry her. He only asked her to watch Susan out of desperation, and because she lived less than one mile away.

"I can't wait to meet Susan." Kelli hadn't held a baby since the last one was adopted from the Orphan Train. Her arms ached for a little one again, but in the meantime she offered to help Carter. "What can I do first? Can I help you bring in some of the supplies?"

"This is the last of it." Carter set the box he was holding down on the floor. "Let me show you the rest of the house before Charlie wakes up and wants to go fishing or to see the cow." He chuckled.

An adorable giggle escaped Kelli's lips. "He is so excited about everything here." Kelli hesitated a moment, chewing her bottom lip. Perhaps Carter did not really want to have to deal with Charlie so much. She wanted to assure Carter that she did not expect him to spend all his time with the boy.

"If you want me to set Charlie straight right away, just tell me how much time you want to spend with him. I don't want him to be under foot if that will bother you. He is a good helper and I don't mind having him around, so don't be afraid to tell me to keep him in here. He will gladly stay with me."

Carter searched Kelli's face for a moment, wondering if she did not want him to try and form a relationship with the boy. He couldn't tell from her expression.

"Kelli, I'm just as excited about having Charlie here as he is about being here. I'm looking forward to spending a lot of time with him. He is my son now. My biggest concern is getting to know what he can and cannot do because of his leg brace."

Kelli gazed at her husband gratefully and then turned away before he could see the look in her eyes change. She was happy that he felt this way about Charlie, but she wanted him to feel that way about her as well. She blinked her eyes, fighting back the tears that threatened to spill over.

Stop being so selfish, she reminded herself again. L*ove does not envy.*

"Charlie can do anything he sets his mind to do, but he knows his limitations. He won't get involved in anything he knows he won't be able to do well."

"Okay then, I will enjoy having him with me. I'll learn what he can do as we go along." Carter picked up the box of supplies and headed towards the other end of the house. Kelli followed. Off the opposite end of the big room was a short hallway leading into the kitchen. It was a small kitchen, in comparison to the large one at the orphanage, but of course, she wouldn't be cooking for a hundred children, so she did not need a big room.

Kelli looked around the kitchen. There was no stove, so she assumed she would be doing the cooking in the large fireplace that was built into one of the walls. She did not have any experience cooking in a fireplace, but she was determined to learn. She wanted to become the best cook that Carter had ever known. She wondered if Abby had been a good cook. She had often heard the old saying; t*he way to a man's heart is through his stomach.*

"I'm not much of a cook," Carter interrupted her thoughts, "but I can make us something for now."

"No, that is my job. I'm anxious to begin."

"Have you ever cooked in a fireplace before?"

Kelli shook her head and chewed her lower lip while she stood staring at the fireplace. "At the orphanage, I often helped out in the kitchen. I was considered a pretty good cook. I'm not sure how I will do here. It is all so different, but why don't you let me look around and see what you have, and I can get something started. Just set all the supplies on the table."

Carter set a box he was holding onto the table. He frowned at the large fireplace. A memory flashed through his mind; a picture of Abby bent over, stirring a bowl of stew. It wasn't a pleasant memory. She hated cooking over the open fire and she complained about it on a regular basis.

"I was meaning to get a real stove before…"

Kelli saw the look flicker in Carter's eyes. She now recognized it as an expression of pain when he remembered something about his first wife. She moved across the room and touched his arm. "This will be fine. I've read books about roughing it in the west. I've always dreamed of this life. You just show me how to light a fire in this old fireplace and watch me! I'm ready for this adventure."

"You won't think that after a few days; once you see all the work it takes to survive here. It is a hard life."

What have I done? Carter questioned himself. *Why did I bring another woman out to this farm? It is no life for a woman.*

"I'm used to hard work." Kelli pushed playfully against his arm, pulling him once again out of his reverie. "Now, why don't you go find something else to do, while I get acquainted with this kitchen?"

Carter hesitated then nodded. "Okay, I'll finish putting the supplies away out in the barn, but I will get the fire going before I leave." He was determined to make things as easy for Kelli as possible.

Kelli watched as Carter built a small fire, carefully observing him and trying to remember each thing he did so that she would be able to make up the fire without any help.

"If there is anything else you want me to help you with, just let me know." Carter was a bit hesitant to leave her in the house alone, especially on her first day here.

"I will."

"There is a dinner calling bell by the porch. If you need anything at all, just ring it."

Kelli stared at him with a blank look on her face and then asked, "What is a dinner calling bell?"

Carter smirked. "Follow me city gal."

Kelli slunk behind him, embarrassed. There were so many things she was going to have to learn. She hoped that Carter would be patient with her. She scuttled up closer, willing to learn everything quickly.

Carter walked out onto the porch, picked up a metal rod and started banging it one the inside a triangular shaped metal rod that was hung on the porch. It made a loud ringing sound.

"That is a dinner bell." Carter handed the long rod to Kelli and told her to give it a try. The first time it barely made any sound at all.

"A little harder," Carter encouraged. Kelli tried again and this time was rewarded with the resounding noise.

"I can hear that pretty much anywhere on the farm. Only ring it for meals or emergencies."

Kelli agreed.

Carter stepped off the porch and moved towards the buckboard. "I'll work on these supplies."

*****

Kelli watched him lead the horses away from the house. *Time to get to work,* she told herself and spent the next half hour peeking into cupboards, drawers, nooks and crannies, until she felt that she knew where everything she needed for cooking was kept. Aside from a stove, there wasn't anything she could think of that wasn't in this kitchen. Set beside the fireplace was a cast iron cauldron and a three legged pan that Carter had called a *Spider.* He explained that the three legged pan was used to stand up in the coals and ashes of the fire. Kelli found a set of pewter dishes as well and used them to set the table with.

Kelli was intrigued when she discovered the room at the back of the house that had been the old Soddy. It was dark and cool. She found that Carter kept some eggs and bacon there. She also found a can of bacon grease on one counter. She gathered several eggs and a few slices of the bacon and turned back to take on the challenge of cooking in the fireplace.

It did not take long for her to put together a quick meal. It was interesting but tricky to cook in a big skillet over the open fire. She noted that there was flour, baking powder, salt, and sugar, so if Carter would bring in some milk, she could probably make biscuits for the morning.

When the food was ready, Kelli made her way to the big front room. Carter had not returned yet. She moved down the hallway and stuck her head into Charlie's room.

"Time to wake up now, Charlie."

The boy opened his eyes, a look of confusion on his face. He sat up and glanced around the room.

"I didn't know where I was for a minute, Kelli."

"Yes, you might feel that way for a few days. Come along now and have something to eat."

Charlie bounded off the bed and followed after her. On the way back to the kitchen, Kelli stepped out onto the front porch and showed Charlie the dinner bell. She gave him the rod and told him to try it. Charlie got it right on the first try.

They were so engaged with the bell that neither of them noticed Carter quickly approaching. When he stepped up beside Kelli she jumped.

"Oh, I didn't know you were here."

"Where you calling me with the bell?"

"I was going to call you with it, but I wanted Charlie to try it first."

"I was already on my way in," Carter explained. "What do you think of the bell, Charlie?"

"It's great." The boy rang it again.

"Whoa there!" Carter reached over and took the rod from the boy's hand. "That's enough for now. In the future, only ring the bell for meals and emergencies."

"Okay, Pa." Charlie answered obediently, but his eyes lingered on the bell. "Can this be one of my jobs?"

Carter ruffled the boys hair. "Sure, whenever you are in the house helping, you can be in charge of ringing the bell."

"I've got some food ready," Kelli interrupted the conversation.

"I'm hungry as a bear…grooowl" Carter lifted his hands in the air, imitating a bear. Charlie and Kelli laughed.

"I'm hungry as a bear too," Charlie said and did his best to imitate a bear as well.

Kelli shook her head. "Alright you bears, wash your paws and come to the table." She turned and headed for the kitchen. Her heart felt so light. Watching Charlie and Carter joke together, made her happy. This is what she wanted for Charlie.

When Carter and Charlie arrived in the kitchen, with clean hands, Kelli had the food set out on the table. "Sit down and let's eat."

Carter rubbed his hands together in anticipation. "Great! All I've had so far today is a glass of lemonade."

Kelli smiled.

Carter chuckled, remembering why he had ended up drinking lemonade in town. "Sit down with us Kelli, I'm sure you are hungry too."

Kelli realized that Charlie and she only had the lemonade as well. Just thinking about it caused rumbling sounds in her stomach. Carter looked down at her with his casual grin.

"I was right."

A red blush rose in her cheeks and she brushed past him. Charlie was already sitting at the table. Carter joined him. The food smelled wonderful. It had been a long, time since he had tasted any good home cooked food. Abby had not been much of a cook. Carter grabbed a bowl and started to serve himself. Kelli wasn't sure how to react, but out of pure shock she gasped, "Don't you pray before you eat?"

Carter's hand went still. It was strange to have his behavior questioned, in his own house, but when he looked at his new wife, remembering she had been raised by nuns, he felt it was a fair question. She must assume that everyone prayed over their meal.

"When my wife was alive I did, but now, well...." Carter didn't finish his statement. He wanted to tell her that since Abby died he just didn't feel very close to God. As a matter of fact, he had been so angry with God that he had almost turned completely away from Him. But time had healed his anger and recently he had been silently offering up prayers again. He just wasn't sure that he wanted to pray out loud, in front of a woman who was still almost a stranger.

Kelli's shoulders sagged. Once again the issue of faith had arisen and she still had no idea if Carter was a Christian or not. By his hesitance to pray, she had to believe that he wasn't.

Oh Lord, what have I done? What kind of marriage have I jumped into?

"I'll pray," Charlie suggested. This seemed to be a solution for now. Both grown-ups agreed and bowed their heads.

"Dear God, thank-you for the food that Kelli made and thank-you God for letting me and Kelli get adopted by Carter. Oh yeah, God, help me to be good at milking cows."

Carter and Kelli burst out laughing. The young boy's honest prayer broke the ice in the room and they both sat back feeling more comfortable.

"This looks great, let's dig in." Carter set the platter down in front of Charlie. The young boy's hand shot out and grabbed up a piece of bacon. Kelli reminded him to use his manners, but she did not scold him because she knew that he was very hungry. Carter filled his plate up.

Kelli watched his face anxiously, as he took his first bite of her cooking. She was concerned when surprise registered on his countenance, but that was quickly replaced by a look of pure ecstasy. He did not have to say anything, she could see that he liked her food.

Carter gobbled down his first bite and filled his fork up with a second. "This is excellent, Kelli," he told her, before shoveling the next bite in. Kelli was delighted.

"Thank-you." She bowed her head to hide the flush that crept into her cheeks.

Charlie watched the two of them for a moment. "What's the matter, Kelli?"

"Nothing, Charlie. Go ahead and eat up." Kelli covered up her embarrassment by reaching over and lifting the platter of food. She served herself.

Charlie knew when to leave Kelli alone, so he cocked his head sideways and said, "You like the food, Pa?"

"Sure do, Son. It's about the best food I've ever tasted. Reminds me of my own mother's cooking."

Kelli was very pleased at his statement, glad that he had not compared it to his late wife's cooking. She lifted her own fork and began to eat contentedly.

******

"Tell us more about how you first came to live here" Charlie begged. Carter did not want to interrupt their first meal with stories that his new family might not be interested in hearing about, but he noticed that Kelli was looking at him with as much eager curiosity as Charlie.

"It's a long story, are you sure you want to hear it now?" His eyes held Kelli's. She nodded.

Carter told tell them about traveling on the wagon train. He skipped over how he and Abby had met, and fell in love. He told about the first year that Abby and he came to this land, and the hardships they endured. Kelli and Charlie listened with wide eyes, enthralled by his story. It never even occurred to Kelli to feel jealous as Carter spoke about Abby, and Carter was so caught up in the story, he never thought about how Kelli must feel when he spoke of his first wife. It actually felt good to talk about his early years of marriage. He had been dwelling on the last few months for so long, that he had almost forgotten about the times when Abby was enthusiastic about their life in Kansas.

Of course, that was only because she wanted me to make a lot of money so we could move back east, Carter reflected, but did not speak his thoughts out loud. He shook his head trying to rid himself of those thoughts.

"I was lucky. My crops did not fail like those of many others who tried to settle in this area. We began to prosper right away. It did not take long before I was able to buy the lumber to build this house. Many other farmers have stone houses, but I wanted mine to be made of wood."

"I'm sure that your wife must have loved it!" Kelli looked around. This home was more magnificent than any she had ever read about. She would have been content to have lived in a Soddy however. In her mind, anything was better than the cramped quarters of the orphanage.

Carter coughed. "Well, not really. She did not like the new house any better than the Soddy."

Charlie looked aghast. "What didn't she like about it? This is a great house."

Kelli looked confused too.

"Abby did not like anything about Kansas." Carter's voice dropped low. "All she wanted, was to go back east. Her parents had forced her to go along on the wagon train with them, even though she wanted to stay in her home town. She begged them to leave her behind, but they just couldn't see leaving a young woman on her own like that, so she was forced into the trip. For a while she thought that marrying me would make her happy, but when we split off from the wagon train to settle here, the reality of the harsh life she was forced to live was too much for her. She could not stand it."

Kelli noticed the sad look in Carter's eyes.

"I tried to make her happy, I really thought that the house would solve our problems. But by time I got it built, she had become so maudlin. Even when we found out she was in the family way, that did not make her happy."

Kelli couldn't help but reach over and pat Carter's arm.

"I wasn't able to stay with her all the time because I had to work and I did not know that she wasn't eating. I thought she was just tired because of the baby, but I was wrong. She grew weaker and weaker. By time the baby came, she was unable to care for herself at all. I had to stop working and I stayed with her all the time. I tried to coax her to eat, for me, for the baby, but it did no good. Giving birth used up all the strength she had left." Carter's voice dropped very low.

Kelli knew that if they continued this conversation, Carter would grow distressed and close up once more. She did not want him to relive that terrible time, so she interrupted him.

"Eat up everyone, before the food gets too cold."

Carter shook himself out of his mood and smiled at her. He was glad she had stopped him from saying anymore. There were some things that needed to be forgotten. Carter picked up his fork and dug into the food again. They all ate silently for a few more minutes. Kelli peeked at Carter and Charlie as they ate. Her heart filled with joy to think that she was now a part of this small family.

Thank-you Lord, for giving me this family. Show me the way to be the best wife and mother I can be.

Carter's voice unexpectedly boomed out, interrupting Kelli's thoughts. "Who wants to come see the cow when we are finished eating? We may even have time for a milking lesson."

Charlie bounced up and down in his seat, eyes sparkling with enthusiasm. "I do, I do!"

"Okay son, finish up your food. What about you Kelli?" His eyes sought hers.

"I can stay in and clean things up." Kelli wasn't really sure she wanted to get to know the cow. From the train window she had seen many cows, but in her eyes they looked so enormous. In New York she had been afraid of the large horses that pulled the milk wagon and from what she could tell, cows weren't much smaller than a horse. "You boys just run along and see the cow."

"We can all clean this up later, together. I think you should join us now. I don't want to let Charlie get too close to the cow if you aren't comfortable with it. You know him better than me." Carter's eyes slipped down to Charlie's leg. He wasn't sure exactly what the boy could or could not do and he did not want to put Charlie into a situation that he wasn't ready for. Kelli understood the look and quickly stood up to go along with them.

He is so kind, Kelli reflected.

As they made their way to the barn, Kelli felt strange. Leaving the dishes on the table was something she had never done before. In the orphanage, Kelli would never have walked away from a dirty table or dirty dishes.

Although she no longer wanted to live the same rigid life she had in the orphanage, there were some things she thought proper to do. Washing dishes was one of them.

When they stepped into the barn, Kelli allowed her eyes to adjust to the darkness. The Soddy walls made the whole place feel damp and smell earthy. Kelli was glad after all, that Carter had a real house and not a Soddy. She wasn't sure she would have liked living in a Soddy, although to have a home of her own, she would have made do. For a moment she could understand why Abby may not have liked their first year living here, if the Soddy Carter and Abby had lived in was anything like this barn.

"Look Kelli, there's the cow!" Charlie called out. Carter had to put his hand out to stop the boy from running up to the animal and spooking her.

"Whoa, son. You don't ever run up to a cow," Carter explained.

The boy lowered his eyes and nodded. Carter chucked him under the chin. "I'm not mad, Son, I just don't want you to get hurt. Be patient, I will teach you how to approach her the right way."

Charlie smiled gratefully. Kelli could see hero worship in Charlie's eyes. It worried her, she did not want Charlie to get hurt. At this point she wasn't sure if Carter would really treat Charlie this well all the time. In the past there were several boys who were kind to him for a short time, but once they saw how the brace on his leg affected his ability to keep up, most of them turned away from him. Kelly was afraid that Charlie already adored Carter too much. If Carter were to turn away from him now, it could crush Charlie's spirit.

Carter showed Charlie the best way to walk up to the cow without scaring her. Then he had Charlie practice several times. Kelli stood far away, unwilling to get too friendly with the beast. The animal looked fairly gentle, but Kelli could not grow accustomed to its size.

Carter got out a small stool and a bucket. He placed them near the cow and showed them both how to milk the cow. Kelli absolutely refused to try. Charlie was hesitant at first, but once he was seated happily on the stool and had caused a stream of milk to splash into the bucket, his interest grew more powerful than his fear. Within minutes, Charlie was happily milking the cow. Kelli could see the bliss on the boy's face. She knew that Charlie wanted to be a helper, and milking the cow was something he could do, even with a brace on his leg.

Charlie smiled up at Carter, his face tinged with pride. "Can I do all the milking from now on?"

Carter looked to Kelli for permission. She nodded.

"You sure can, Son. That is one job I will gladly turn over." Carter patted Charlie on the head and patted the cow at the same time.

Charlie's face brightened even more. He turned his attention back to the cow, and began to milk her with a serious determination.

Kelli noted that Carter had called Charlie 'Son' several times. She thought it was wonderful how easily they had become like father and son. She only wondered if she would ever feel like a real wife to Carter.

Carter stood beside her, watching Charlie. She twisted her head slightly and looked up at him. He was a very handsome man; up close he was even more so than she had originally thought. He seemed somehow different here, on his own land, than he had in town. His rugged good looks matched this homestead.

"Kelli, Kelli..." Charlie's voice drew her back from her thoughts.

"Yes, Charlie."

"Can we stay here forever?"

Kelli smiled at the boy. In all the years she had known him, he had never looked so happy. But she did not want to make him any promises. Carter may have married her, but he had the option to give Charlie back to the orphanage if things did not work out. Of course, if he chose to send Charlie back, she would go with the boy, married or not. She had made a commitment to take care of Charlie, before she ever met Carter.

Kelli looked up for a moment.

Lord, can I really promise him that we will stay here forever? Is this really our home?

With a small shoulder shrug, Kelli finally answered the boy. "As long as Carter needs us, we will stay. But I cannot promise you forever."

In his childish acceptance, Charlie squealed, "Oh, as long as there is a cow here, he will need me."

Carter chuckled at the boy's answer. "As long as you can do the milking, I'll need you." He walked over and to show Charlie what to do when the bucket was full.

Kelli stood silently, staring at them. It was such a wonderful thing. Charlie as Carter's son. She chewed her lip, however, and wondered, *will he ever really need me?*

Chapter 6

While Charlie finished milking the cow, Carter showed Kelli around the outside area between the house and the barn. He pointed to the outhouse, which caused Kelli to blush red. When Carter noticed the flush on her cheeks, he turned away with a grin. He had almost forgotten how easily a woman could be brought to a blush. His own wife had been embarrassed about that as well.

Stop thinking about her. Stop comparing her. Kelli is your wife now. Carter forced himself to turn his attention back to his new wife. She seemed eager to learn all about the farm, something Abby had never taken any interest in, and had not cared to learn about.

Carter emphasized certain things that Kelli needed to be careful about. He warned her about many things and showed her several places that were dangerous. He even showed her some of the spots where snakes were known to hide. While he continued his instruction, Carter noticed worry creeping across Kelli's face as she tried to remember all the words of advice. He could tell that some of the warnings frightened her. Not having lived in the country she wasn't used to taking the precautions that were necessary. She wasn't used to watching out for things like snakes. N*either was Abby,* Carter recalled. *I wonder if Kelli will be strong enough to live here. She seems sound, but her skin is so pale. She might not be able to handle country life*. Fear began to rise up in his chest.

"What's wrong Carter?" Kelli had detected the frown furrowing on his brow again. She was already able to read some of his moods based on his facial expressions.

Carter looked away for a moment, waiting for the beating in his heart to stop. His thoughts of Kelli had disturbed him. He berated himself for having acted so selfishly by marrying her. *I shouldn't have married her. I should have noticed how delicate she is. Why did I agree to this crazy marriage?*

When he looked at Kelli again, she smiled, but bit her bottom lip. He could see that she had read the worry on his face. Carter clinched his fists, fighting the emotions that had been stirred up inside him. He was angry at himself for his thoughtless actions that could possibly harm another woman.

"Carter?"

Carter did not want his own mood to cause her any further alarm. "There is absolutely nothing wrong. I was just thinking about all the things a city gal like you doesn't know about."

"I'm willing to learn them."

"That all sounds great, but you really don't know what you have gotten into. Life is very hard here, Kelli. It will not be easy for you to adjust."

"I'm sure it will all work out," Kelli insisted with her dogmatic attitude. "I'm really looking forward to becoming a true country girl."

"It isn't only the things you will have to avoid, and the things you will have to learn; the work here is difficult as well."

"I know that, Carter, but I'm not afraid of hard work."

Carter eyed her again, noting her small frame. It looked as if she could be blown away with just one of the gusts of wind that daily blew across the prairie.

"But are you strong enough and healthy enough to handle it?"

Kelli was sure she knew what made him ask that question; he was comparing her to Abby. Kelli stood up straight. She wanted to help ease Carter's worries.

"Do I look sickly?"

"You are very pale," Carter spoke truthfully.

Kelli gazed at him for a moment. He was not pale at all. He was a lovely, golden brown color; bronzed from the sun. Kelli held out her hands and could see that in comparison to him, she was very pale.

"There wasn't much sunlight in New York; at least not at the orphanage. I spent most of the time inside, teaching or taking care of the babies. I probably only spent about an hour a week outside. That is why my skin is so fair. I have never been sick a day of my life."

"You will get burned here." Carter's voice dropped. He didn't sound very happy about that.

Kelli could see that Carter was more than slightly concerned about the issues he had brought up. She was curious as to why he was suddenly so concerned about her strength and her skin. "Maybe I'll just get tan," she squeaked out in a soothing tone, trying to assure him. She did not want to start out their relationship with him worried about her all the time. She wanted to be a helper, not a hindrance to him.

"We'll see," Carter growled unhappily. The more he thought about the things that Kelli would have to overcome and learn, the more irritated with himself he became. "You will have to wear a bonnet all the time and long sleeves."

"Then I will never get my skin used to the sun."

"You will be surprised how your skin can burn, even if it is covered up."

"It sounds very hot!" Kelli complained, just thinking about wearing clothes that would cover her so much.

"Actually, the long sleeves and the bonnet will protect you from the sun, and help to keep you cool, especially if you are working outside."

"What kind of outside work will I do?" Kelli asked, wanting to change the subject. "Will I work in the fields with you?"

"Not very often, only during the harvest. There is a small garden around the other side of the house. You can work out there each day, when the sun is not too high. That should be a good way for you to get used to the sun."

Kelli's eyes lit up. "A garden? Really? I've always wanted to have a garden. Where is it?"

"Let's check on Charlie first, and then I'll take you to see the garden."

*****

Charlie had just finishing the milking when Kelli and Carter re-entered the barn. His face was lit up with satisfaction.

"Look Kelli, a whole bucket full." Charlie beamed and carried the pail over so that Kelli and Carter could inspect it.

"Wow, that is a lot of milk. You really did a good job."

Carter leaned over and looked into the bucket as well "You sure did. I'm surprised that Daisy was so obliging."

Kelli had to hold back a giggle.

"What's so funny?" Carter asked.

"Why did you name your cow Daisy?"

"That's just what you name a cow, everyone I know has at least one cow named Daisy."

"Oh." Kelli had a hard time imagining a big strapping cowboy like Carter, calling his cow Daisy.

Charlie was chuckling a bit as well. Carter gave them both one of his best no nonsense stares, but it didn't stop them from laughing.

"Okay, if you can both stop laughing now, I would love to show you the garden. You did want to see the garden didn't you?"

Kelli quieted down and forced herself to behave more seriously. "Yes, I would love to see it."

Carter told Charlie to put the bucket of milk in the old Soddy room, at the back of the house, where it would cool. When Charlie headed off, walking slowly, so that the milk would not slosh out of the pail, Carter headed towards the side of the house. Kelli hurried behind him. It was hard to keep up with him when he took full strides, so she had to run a bit.

Because she wasn't watching, Kelli smashed into Carter's back, when he stopped. He turned in surprise. Kelli's hand shot up to cover her mouth in embarrassment. "Oops, I'm sorry." The memory of their meeting in town flashed into her mind. Carter was going to begin to think she was very clumsy.

"No problem." Carter's face showed his amusement. He decided that he liked to see her slightly discomfited, because it put a bit of color into her cheeks.

Charlie came rushing over and rejoined them, eager for the next experience.

"The garden is over here," Carter explained as he led them around the side of the house. In a few moments they all stood beside the small plot of land that had begun to fill with weeds again. Kelli could hardly tell that this had ever been a real garden. It looked more like a small area where a child had played in the dirt.

"It's not much." Carter shook his head sadly. "Abby did not like to get dirty, so she only agreed to a small garden. She insisted we buy most of our food from neighbors or town. We can keep doing that if you really don't like gardening."

"We had a large garden at the orphanage, but I was never assigned to work there. I don't know much about gardening." She stood with hands on hips, contemplating.

"Then you probably won't want to work in a garden here." Kelli heard a tinge of disappointment in Carter's voice. She could see that he was very sensitive about things that his first wife did not like. Kelli hoped that if she tried to be enthusiastic about anything that Abby had not liked, Carter might begin to care for her more.

94

That's not very honest! she thought, as she pushed a tendril of hair off her face. *And besides, I don't want him to care for me more. I just want him to care for me as I am.*

For a few seconds, Kelli stood staring at the garden, thinking about the challenge it would be, but she had never been one to back down from a challenge. It only took moments before she was filled with a true desire to clean up the garden and to grow the best vegetables around. In time, perhaps the neighbors would buy vegetables from her.

"I think that I am going to love working in the garden," Kelli gushed.

Carter's head shot up, a grin plastered on his face.

"But there is one is very small thing I will need.

Carter squinted at her anxiously, wondering what it was she could want. He worried that she would start to demand all sorts of things that he could not provide, the way that Abby had.

"What is that small thing?" Carter tried to sound curious, but the surge of anger he felt could be heard in his tone. Kelli did not notice it because she was busy making plans in her head.

"Oh, nothing very important. I will just need you to expand the garden. It will need to be at least double this size if we really want to grow enough food so that we can put some away for the winter. I've read that women who live on farms, can items they grow, to serve them during the winter months."

A smile flitted across Carter's face.

"I'll get this garden doubled in no time," he assured her. "It is probably too late in the season to grow very much this year, however."

"Yes, but there are some things we can grow fairly quickly, right?"

"I only know about wheat. I think there are a few books about gardening in the house. Abby's mother gave them to her as a wedding gift; not that she ever used them. I think that several of the neighbors will be happy to share canning tips with you."

Neighbors? She hadn't thought about neighbors. Now Kelli wondered if there were other women nearby, willing to share their ideas and help her. She felt a sense of trepidation. Would they laugh at her, and treat her like a child, or even worse, snub her because she was an orphan?

Kelli lifted her chin defiantly at the thought. She would read all the books that Carter had mentioned first, and learn as much as she could. Then, if she needed any extra help from the neighbors, she would gratefully accept it; if they did not mock her.

Carter did not notice Kelli's foreboding. He seemed very pleased with her interest in the garden and promised that he would give her the books that evening.

"I want to show you one more thing before we go inside."

"What?" Charlie's voice chirped.

"I want to show you both the creek."

Charlie had barely ever heard the word creek in his life. There were no creeks in New York City; especially none near the orphanage. "What's a creek?"

"Come along and I will show you. It is our source of fresh water."

As they strolled across the open plain towards the area where Carter said the creek was, Kelli and Carter talked more about the garden. Carter had many suggestions and ideas. Kelli nodded her head in agreement to all of them. She was enjoying being able to talk to her husband. She felt as though they had found something that they could share, without the presence of Abby blocking the way.

"I don't see any water, Pa." Charlie remarked as his eyes scanned the vast fields in front of them.

Carter reached over and patted the boy's shoulder. "It's pretty well hidden by the tall grass. We are almost there."

Charlie looked unconvinced, but continued walking. Even Kelli squinted, trying to discover the whereabouts of the mysterious creek.

Charlie and Kelly were surprised when they finally stepped through the tall grass and found themselves standing on the banks of the creek. They both stood in awe, staring at the gently moving water. Kelli was mesmerized by its beauty. The water was crystal clear.

"What a lovely spot," Kelli sighed. "What kind of rock is that in the creek?"

"The bedrock is limestone and shale."

"Is the water cold?" Charlie asked.

"Take off your shoes and stick your foot in it."

Charlie looked to Kelli. She hesitated.

"Is it safe? Are there any water moccasins in there?" She remembered reading something about them in one of the books she had studied that told all about the west.

"No, just a few fish. They won't come near you."

"Alright then," Kelli agreed.

Charlie whooped in excitement, slipped off his new boots and socks and headed towards the bank.

Carter stared at the metal brace on the boy's leg.

"Is it alright for him to get his brace wet?"

"Probably not. Charlie, you better take your brace off before you put your foot in the water."

"OK." Charlie plopped on the edge of the creek and struggled to undo his brace. Carter began to move forward to help him, but Kelli shook her head and whispered.

"He needs to do it himself."

It wasn't long before Charlie had successfully removed the brace and had slipped his feet into the cool water. He sat happily, wiggling his toes.

"Kelli, it's great! You've got to try it."

Kelli pursed her lips. "I'll take your word for it."

"Can you swim?" Carter asked. Charlie and Kelli turned and gaped at Carter with blank faces.

"I guess that means no. Don't worry, I'll teach you."

"I'm not sure that would be a good idea," Kelli stated.

"Why not?"

"We could get sick from the water..."

"Cold, fresh creek water is good for you, and swimming will make Charlie's legs strong."

Kelli looked doubtful.

"Charlie is pale, so we won't be able to stay in the sun too long today, but we could have our first lesson now."

Kelli sat down and let the water flow over her hand.

"It's too cold."

Carter bent over and felt the water. "It's just right. Wait until winter, then you will feel cold water."

Kelli wasn't sure about getting into the creek water at all. At the orphanage there had been water available for a daily cleaning and once a month everyone took a bath. But the idea of actually plunging into cold water did not seem prudent. Once, she had heard the kitchen cook talking about how her uncle had fallen into a lake. He had died afterward from getting chilled.

"You'll get used to it quickly. It's only cold at first."

Kelli looked dubious.

"You might as well come to terms with the idea, Kelli. We do most of our bathing in the creek too."

"Don't you have a bathtub in the house?"

"Yes. We only use it in the winter, when we can bring in snow to melt. It's too much work to lug all the buckets of water from the creek, into the house."

"Surely once a month wouldn't be too difficult?"

"Once a month?"

"We only took a bath once a month at the orphanage," Kelli informed him.

"What did you do the rest of the time?"

Kelli blushed. This was a very intimate conversation, and even if Carter were her husband, she wasn't ready to talk about such personal matters. She mumbled her answer in embarrassment. "We had a water pitcher and a sponge that we used to clean up with every day."

Carter let out a long whistle. "Well, I sure wouldn't be able to stand myself if I only had a good cleaning once a month. I come down to the creek at least every other day and take a dip. Now in the winter, I heat up buckets of the snow and have a sponge bath daily, and a real bath once a week."

Kelli's lip trembled at the thought. She wondered if Carter would insist that she do that too. By the look on his face she knew he would. She had never considered herself dirty, but standing in front of Carter now, she felt like she had never really fully bathed before. Kelli didn't think her face could turn any deeper crimson than it was right now.

Carter jumped up, looked at the sky and announced. "The sun is going to set soon. I think we have enough time for our first swimming lesson, Charlie."

"Yippee."

"Right now would be a good time to start a habit of getting cleaned up, Kelli. So you go down where the water is a little more shallow. You can slip off your dress and wash it while you bathe. Charlie and I will bathe right here."

Charlie leapt up in excitement. "Should I take off my clothes, too?"

"Yes, but leave your under clothes on."

Charlie started unbuttoning his shirt. Kelli stood horrified.

"I'm not sure about this Carter," she stammered. "Charlie, wait!"

Carter could tell that this was an issue she was going to have to be ram-rodded into accepting.

"Okay, Kelli. If you don't mind that you smell, I can accept that, but Charlie and I are gonna get good and clean right now."

Carter unbuttoned his shirt and pulled it off. He knew that his action would shock her. Although he had on long johns under his shirt and pants, he could see that Kelli was totally embarrassed. She turned her back on them quickly, determined not to submit to his crazy idea about bathing in the cold creek.

Carter watched her turn away. He noted her statue-like stance. He chuckled a bit and shook his head. Carter picked Charlie up and carried the boy into the water.

Charlie giggled and whooped as Carter dipped him into the water to get his body used to the cold temperature. After a while, Charlie yelled for Kelli to jump in.

"It's not really that cold, once you get used to it, Kelli."

Kelli stood still for several minutes. She could hear them splashing in the water behind her. Charlie's voice rang out with pleasure. Kelli was angry that Carter had put her in this situation. She had always been in charge of Charlie. He had never been allowed to disobey her before. She wanted to insist that Charlie obey her, but Carter was his father now.

101

Kelli stood silently listening. It did sound like he was having fun and Kelli wanted Charlie to be happy.

The sun beat down on her head and Kelli could feel sweat beads form on her forehead. Although she did not believe that she smelled, she lifted her arm and sniffed. She still wasn't sure that she smelled, but she could tell that her dress was a bit musty from the train ride. It would be nice to wash it.

Kelli thought about it a bit more. If by chance she did smell, Carter was not going to like it. She knew that if she was ever going to convince Carter to make her his real wife, she would need him to like the way she looked and the way she smelled.

Finally, she stomped her foot in aggravation and began to wander towards the shallow section of the creek that Carter had pointed out to her. She sat down on the bank and slipped off her shoes and socks, then tentatively slipped her foot into the cool water. It felt very refreshing.

Kelli bent over, cupped her hands, filled them with the cool water, and splashed her face. It felt heavenly. She had not realized just how warm she really did feel. She could hear Charlie laughing, so she peeked over to see if they were watching her. When she was sure that they had their backs turned to her, she stood up and started to slip off her dress. Her face flamed at the thought of Carter seeing her badly tattered under garments, so once she was out of her dress, she quickly slipped into the water, hoping he had not been watching and had not noticed.

The water was cold, but revitalizing. It was only about two feet deep so Kelli was able to sit down completely in it.

This is much better than just splashing my face with water!

Kelli scrubbed at her face, then her arms and legs. It did feel wonderful to be completely clean. Her last bath had been a day or two before they had left the orphanage, and she had not been able to clean up very well on the train.

When she finished bathing, Kelli turned and sat watching Carter and Charlie splashing around. The water was deeper in the area where they were, but only another foot or so. She did not have to worry about Charlie, he was able to stand in the water, even with his weak leg.

Kelli was intrigued to see Carter take Charlie in his arms and hold him on the top of the water. Each time he told Charlie to kick his legs. Charlie did the best he could, but his legs were weak. Carter kept encouraging him however.

For a moment Carter looked over in Kelli's direction and noticed her watching them. He was glad to see that she had finally taken his advice and gotten into the water.

"Dunk your head under the water," Carter called over to Kelli. "Nothing fresher than creek-washed hair."

Kelli sat absolutely still. She was not going to dunk her head under the water. She was afraid she would drown. She hoped that Carter would turn away and forget about her, but Carter had begun to walk towards Kelli. Charlie crawled along the bottom of the creek behind him.

When Carter reached her side, Kelli turned her eyes away. Carter did not seem discomfited to have Kelli see him in his wet long johns, but Kelli was totally embarrassed to have him see her in her undergarments. Kelli quickly wrapped her arms tightly across her chest and sank down into the water as far as she could.

"You gonna dunk your head?" Carter asked as he sat down right beside her.

"No, I don't want to drown!"

Carter put an arm out behind her. She could feel his arm brush across her back. "Kelli, just lay your head back on my arm. You will be able to float. I won't let you drown and that way your hair will get clean too."

"You can trust him, Kelli," Charlie assured her. "He's real strong. He held me up in the water and I never once drowned."

Kelli laughed. She turned and looked at Carter. He was no longer laughing or playing. He was very serious.

"You can trust me, Kelli."

Kelli slipped her head back until she was lying on his arm in the water. She could feel the water swirling through her hair. Carter told her to stretch the rest of her body out more, and as she did her body began to float. Carter kept one arm under her head and another under her back.

"Doesn't that feel nice," Carter's voice sounded husky, but when she looked at him, he had his face turned away.

"Yes, it does. I suppose I could stand this a few times a week, if you really think it's okay." After a few minutes Kelli sat back up and Carter dropped his arm. For a moment he just sat staring at her; with her hair hanging down around her shoulders and the sun splashing through it, she was more beautiful than he had thought at first. She was very young looking, but she looked old enough to....to...kiss. Carter started to lean closer to her but Kelli pulled away and wrapped her arms in front of herself again.

She had not noticed his intentions.

What am I doing? Carter sat back in the water and gazed at her. His stomach tightened when he thought about kissing her. It did not matter that she was his wife now, he knew that was only in name.

Kelli wondered what he was thinking.

"Do I smell better now?" she asked.

Carter shook himself out of his reverie and leaned over playfully, making a long sniffing sound. "I guess you'll do for. Next time we can bring some soap."

"Oooh, you!" Kelli splashed water at him. Carter just chuckled. Kelli liked the sound that rumbled through him.

"We better all get going, you two pale skins have had enough sun for one day," Carter announced. "Come on, Son."

Carter and Charlie made their way back to the place where their clothes were stacked. Carter taught Charlie how to rinse the clothes in the water. While they scrubbed their clothing, Kelli slipped up to the edge and retrieved her own dress. It could use a good cleaning as well. So within minutes, all three of them were happily washing their clothes.

It wasn't until they finished that Kelli realized that they had no way to dry the clothes or their own bodies for that matter. She saw Carter and Charlie spread their clothes out on some bushes to dry. She dragged herself closer to the edge and spread her dress out on the branches of a small scrub bush that grew beside the creek.

"It will take hours for these clothes to dry," Carter called over to her. "I think if we slip on our shoes we can all dry off at the house. Go ahead, Kelli, we will follow behind you."

"But, but…" Kelli hesitated. She didn't want to explain to Carter that her under garments had holes in them that she did not want him to see. "I think that I need to rinse my skirt one more time. You two go ahead and I will follow in just a minute."

Carter and Charlie sat on the edge of the creek and slipped their socks and shoes on. Charlie was shivering, so he needed help putting on his leg brace. Carter was rather clumsy, trying to help Charlie. Kelli noted that Charlie's head hung down dejectedly, but Carter finally chucked him under the chin.

"Sorry about that, Son. This is new to me, but I'll get the hang of it."

"That's okay, Pa," Charlie answered and his cheeks burned in shame.

Carter sat next to Charlie and put his arm around him.

"Charlie, I had a horse once that hurt his leg. The other farmers told me to shoot him. But, I built a special sling that kept all the weight off his leg. I rubbed it with ointment and I exercised it every day. Over time his leg got stronger and stronger. It wasn't long before he was able to walk again. Then I started making him walk and run in the creek and before you know it, his leg was so strong I was able to ride him again."

"Really?" Charlie's eyes lit up. "Do you think my leg could get strong like that?"

Kelli lifted her head. She wanted to hear the answer to Charlie's question. She had never considered that his leg could get better. At the orphanage, no one seemed to care about trying to help him. Kelli had always just assumed that Charlie would need to wear a leg brace for his entire life.

Carter thought about his answer. "I don't know, but we can sure try. Maybe if your legs get strong from swimming you won't need your brace."

Carter enjoyed seeing the excitement in Charlie's eyes, but he didn't want to give the boy false hope. Carter did not know that much about Charlie's leg problems and a small boy was not the same as a horse.

"We can try."

"I'll work real hard. I want to be strong. I want to be a good helper for you."

Carter could see the determination in Charlie.

"I would love to see your leg get stronger, but you need to understand that you are my son now; with a leg brace or without, I am going to love you just as you are." Carter reached out for the boy.

A tear slipped down Kelli's cheek as she saw Charlie dive his head into Carter's chest for a hug.

Carter reached up and wiped his eyes. Kelli was sure that he had been on the verge of tears.

Carter looked over the boy's bent head at Kelli and smiled. Kelli mouthed the words, "Thank-you."

Chapter 7

In the room that Carter had given her to share with the baby, Kelli ran a brush through her hair as she reflected on her first day as a married woman. She knew that it was not exactly the kind of marriage that most girls dreamed about, but so far she could tell that her life in Kansas was going to be much nicer than the life she had lived at the orphanage. Of course, she knew that it would be hard work, taking care of the baby and Charlie, cooking all the meals and doing the other chores like cleaning and laundry plus working in a garden, but Kelli was used to hard work.

"And I'll be a lot cleaner too," she giggled, thinking about her experience in the creek. Just the thought brought the red hue back to her cheeks. Carter had not seen her undergarments because she had stayed behind him and Charlie, but next time he might. She was going to have to do something about that as soon as possible. She wasn't sure if the material Carter had picked at the general store would work to make herself new undergarments, but she would have to solve the problem with whatever she had.

Since her skirt was still outside drying, Kelli opened her traveling bag and pulled out the only other item she owned. It too was made of heavy wool. Just the idea of putting it on made Kelli cringe. Now that she had felt the cool creek water, she dreaded wearing something so warm.

While she was looking over her meager wardrobe and debating what to do, Carter knocked on her door. Kelli whipped her head around and pulled a quilt up in front of her, afraid that Carter might just open the door and step in the room. She held her breath for a moment and waited. Carter knocked again.

"Yes?" Kelli called out.

"I have a package here with some things I think you could use." Carter's voice was muffled behind the closed door. Kelli looked around for a place to hide in case he decided to open the door and bring the package in. She remained silent.

"Can you open the door a crack and let me hand you the package?" Carter asked. After a moment or two she realized that he was not going to actually invade her space so she stepped over to the door and slipped it open enough for him to stick his arm through. There was a bundle in his extended hand. Kelli took it.

"Open it before you get dressed." Kelli pushed the door closed again. She held the bundle out as if it were a snake. She could not imagine what Carter would give her that she would need before she got dressed. She stared at the package for a full minute.

This is silly, she thought. *I won't know what is in the package until I open it.*

Finally, she set the brown wrapped package on the end of the bed. She reached out and untied the strings that were loosely wrapped around it. Once the strings were off the packing paper slipped open to reveal new bloomers. In fact there were several of them. Kelli was amazed at how soft they were. She had never owned anything like them before. Most of the undergarments she owned were hand made from old flour sacks that the cook used at the orphanage, and she had never owned more than two of those at a time. This package contained enough for her to have a new set to wear every other day for a week. Kelli picked them up one by one and admired them.

110

It astounded her that Carter had known exactly what she needed. Of course, he had been married before and he probably knew a lot more about what a woman would need in the country than she did. Still, the idea of him choosing the feminine items for her was very embarrassing. She wondered how she would ever face the man at the general store again.

Kelli set the bloomers aside. In the package there were also several lengths of ribbon that she could use to tie back her hair.

"There's some dresses hanging in the closet for you as well," Carter called through the door which made her jump up and pull the quilt in front of her again. She stood still and waited until she heard Carter's footsteps moving away from her room. When she was sure that he was gone, she turned and quickly rushed to the closet, which was really just a corner of the room with a sheet strung up in front of it. She pulled the sheet to the side and gasped.

Kelli discovered three very nice calico dresses hanging there. Carter had asked her which one she liked at the general store and she had admitted to liking the blue one best, but she had never expected him to buy the ready made dress for her. She had not been watching what he bought very closely, so she did not notice that he had added three dresses to the pile and the undergarments. Kelli reached in and pulled the china blue calico out, and slipped it over her head. The material was much thinner than the heavy wool skirt she had worn all the way from the orphanage. She felt light and free. The new undergarments were soft, not itchy like those from the orphanage. She felt like a fairy princess. These were the finest clothes she had ever worn.

Kelli spun around in a circle. She had never felt so unencumbered by her clothing before. *I will never wear my wool skirt again,* she decided, but then remembered what she had read about the cold winters in Kansas. She would have to put the skirt away and save it for the colder months. Kelli looked back at the other two dresses. One was a lovely yellow calico and the other a soft green color. Carter must have hung them in the room while she had been walking slowly back to the house from the creek.

He is so kind. If only he really wanted me as his wife. I could be so happy.

Kelli was barefoot, but the floor of the house was smooth wood, so she wasn't worried about splinters. When they had returned from the creek, Carter told her to set her shoes and stocking outside her door and he would place them near the fire to dry. Kelli finished tying a ribbon in her hair, set the brush down on the dresser and moved towards the door. Before she stepped out of the room, she smiled and whispered a small prayer.

Thank-you, Lord, for bringing me to this beautiful home, and giving me these beautiful clothes. This must be part of the good plans You have for me.

Kelli made her way down the hall and out into the large front room. She walked up to the chairs by the fireplace where Carter was sitting. He had lit a small fire and all of their shoes and stockings were spread out on the floor near by. When Carter heard her softly shuffle across the floor, he looked up. Kelli saw his face light up. He pointed to the other chair by the fire, indicating that she should sit down. Kelli sat. She hoped that they could talk for a while and get to know one another better.

"You look very nice in that dress," he told her, but his eyes said much more. He was amazed at how completely different she looked now. In the new dress, with her hair brushed out, pulled back gently off her face and tied with a ribbon, she was one of the most lovely women he had ever seen.

"This dress is so light and..." Kelli stopped talking as a flush swept over her cheeks again. "Thank-you for the other items," she mumbled in embarrassment.

"Sure," Carter dragged his eyes off her reluctantly. Dressed in the blue calico, she was far more lovely than he could have ever imagined. For a moment, a touch of guilt filled his soul, because it had slipped into his mind that Kelli was even more lovely than his first wife. Abby had been a true beauty; polished and refined, but Kelli had a different type of beauty. She was more like the beauty that he saw every day on the Kansas prairie; a wild and free kind of beauty.

Kelli felt self conscious sitting across from Carter. She was uncomfortable because he seemed to be staring right through her and he did not speak. She closed her eyes for a moment, enjoying the warmth of the flames. In her entire life, she had never felt such total peace before.

Carter kept glancing at Kelli, trying to convince himself that it was only the trick of the firelight that made her so attractive, so inviting...

Just as Kelli was beginning to feel relaxed and ready for a nice long chat with her new husband, Carter stood up abruptly. "I best go get the baby," he announced, stomping over and grabbing his boots. Kelli looked out the window.

"But it's dark out."

"I can see my way by the light of the moon."

While Carter slammed his boots on, the smile on Kelli's face fell. She had hoped they could spend some time just getting to know one another before he brought Susan home. Once the baby was in the house, there would be little time for her and Carter to talk privately. Right now, Charlie was in his room happily playing with a set of wooden farm animals that Carter had given him, so Kelli thought that it would have been a perfect time for them to converse. There were so many questions she wanted to ask him.

When he had invited her to sit down, she thought that he wanted to talk. She could not understand his abrupt behavior now.

"Alright," Kelli answered unenthusiastically. Carter noticed her shoulders sag. He felt bad about rushing off so quickly, but he needed to get away. He needed to keep his mind off of Kelli. He needed to remember his love for Abby.

"I will prepare our evening meal while you are gone." Carter saw a few tears begin to brim in Kelli's eyes. Her eyes were really quite delightful and he hated to see the sadness that had filled them, but he just could not stop himself. He had to get away from her, had to clear his head.

Carter turned and stormed out the door, angry at himself for his thoughts. Before he opened the front door, he turned to Kelli and gruffly said, "I'll be back in an hour." Kelli felt a jolt all the way through her soul when the door slammed behind him.

A tear slipped down her cheek as she sat alone by the cheerful fire. She wondered why Carter had suddenly become so angry and distant. She was hurt by his behavior.

At first, he had seemed genuinely pleased when he noticed her in the new dress. She could not imagine what she had done to upset him. She tried to review the scene in her mind, but could think of nothing she had done or said that would have caused Carter to behave in such a manner. It bothered her because she wanted to be able to understand her husband and his moods, but so far she felt like she was stumbling around in the dark.

Sister Marter had always told her that girls were highly emotional, but from what she could see, Carter seemed more so than herself. While she sat thinking, she tried to decide what she could do about Carter's strange behavior, but she could think of nothing else to do about it except turn it over to God. Kelli slipped out of the chair and knelt on the fur rug in front of the fire.

Dear Lord, please help me to understand Carter. I want to be a good wife to him. I want to be a real wife to him. I know that he loved his first wife, but Lord, I'm asking You to help him to love me as well.

Kelli sat quietly for a time basking in the warmth of the fire and the sweet closeness she felt with the Lord. When she stood up, she knew that God had heard her prayer and would answer her in His own time. She just needed to be patient and kind to Carter.

Kelli walked around the room, taking a closer look at several of the objects that she had only glanced at earlier. One thing she was happy to see was a Bible tucked into a shelf with several other books that she would like to read. She pulled the Bible out and opened it. On the page were names. She followed the list to the bottom. The last two names were Carter and Susan.

Kelli caressed the book. The pages were well worn. Kelli hoped that meant that at some time in his life Carter had read the book. She took the Bible and placed it on the small table beside the chair where Carter had been sitting earlier. She would have to talk to him about his faith soon. Perhaps she could encourage him to read some of the stories from the well-loved book to Charlie. That was something she could remember that her father used to do.

"Whatcha doing?" Charlie popped into the room startling Kelli.

"Oh, just looking around at everything. Are you tired of playing already?"

"No, just hungry."

"I think we could find something. You probably worked up a big appetite doing all that swimming in the creek."

Charlie nodded "I can't wait to go in the water again. I wish the kids from the orphanage could have a creek. "

Kelli nodded her head in agreement. Fresh air and sunshine would have been nice at the orphanage as well.

"Do you really think my leg could get strong, Kelli?" A frown creased Charlie's brow.

"I hope so, Charlie. Carter thinks it could. You should pray about it and see what God has to say."

"I will, but if it doesn't get better, do you think that Carter will still like me?"

"Of course he will. Didn't he tell you that your leg brace didn't matter? Doesn't he already let you call him Pa?" Kelli bent over and hugged the boy's small frame.

"Yes, but a real Pa wants to be proud of his son. If my leg doesn't get stronger, I won't be able to do much more around the farm than milk the cow. There won't be anything for him to be proud of."

Kelli gazed at the young boy who bore such wise eyes. "Charlie, there are many things in life you will do to make Carter and I proud of you, not only things on the farm. There will be school; you've always been good at your studies, and there is still a lot about the Bible you need to learn. If you learn to be a good and godly man, I know I will be very proud of you."

"But what about Carter?"

"I'm sure all those things will make him proud as well, and I also think that he will be proud of the way you take care of your new little sister."

Charlie thought it over and finally agreed. He decided that no matter what happened with his leg, he would work hard at everything he did and that way Carter was sure to be proud of him and want to continue to be his Pa.

And as long as there is a cow to milk, he'll want me.

"Where is Pa anyways?" Charlie questioned.

"He went to get the baby."

"I want to be the best big brother in the world." A troubled look snuck into the boy's eyes.

"Charlie, you have always been wonderful with babies. I just know you will make a great brother for Susan. Now why don't we get you something to eat?"

Kelli headed to the kitchen and Charlie followed with a small backwards glance. He wanted to look around the room more, there were so many interesting things to see, but his desire for food was stronger.

Kelli noticed the way Charlie's eyes had scanned the room, so once she had served Charlie a small glass of milk and a piece of bread, she sat down in the chair next to him and said, "Charlie, there are many new and interesting things in this house."

Charlie nodded in agreement.

"I'm sure that you are curious about them all."

"I am, but I'm not sure what I can or cannot touch. I'm afraid I might break something and then Carter will be mad at me."

"I understand your feelings. How would it be if you and I explore together? Each day we will spend a little time looking at all the interesting items in the house. I will watch over you and make sure that nothing really fragile gets broken."

Charlie's face lit up with enthusiasm. "That sounds great, Kelli." In a few minutes Charlie had finished his milk and bread, but Kelli could tell he was still hungry.

"That will hold you until Carter gets back and we can eat a real meal," she assured him, although he looked doubtful.

Kelli laughed at the soulful expression on his face. Charlie could make anyone in the world feel sorry for him with just a small frown. "Okay, Okay! Enough of the poor pitiful look. You will survive until we can eat with Carter. Do you want to help me make some biscuits?"

"Sure!"

The two of them spent a happy hour baking. They talked about good memories they had in common and about the many wonderful sights they had seen since coming west on the Orphan Train.

"I kept praying I'd get adopted, but God knew I didn't really mean it," Charlie explained to Kelli.

"What do you mean?"

"Well, I wanted a family of my own, but I didn't want to leave you. Isn't it great the way that God worked it out so that I could get adopted and still be with you?"

A small tear slipped out of Kelli's eye. "Yes, I would call it a very special miracle."

*****

It was an hour before they finally heard the wagon pull up outside. Charlie was sitting at the kitchen table cutting out the biscuits from the dough that Kelli had prepared.

"He's back!" Charlie jumped up and started to lunge towards the door, but Kelli stopped him.

"No, Charlie, just sit back down."

"Why? I want to see the baby."

"So do I, but we should wait until Carter brings her in."

Charlie fixed his eyes on Kelli for a moment. He was very sensitive and could tell she was nervous about something.

"Okay." Charlie clambered back onto the chair obediently. "Are you worried about taking care of the baby? You shouldn't be. You know everything about babies."

"I'm not nervous." Kelli hesitated a moment. There had to be a reason that she felt a huge lump in her throat. "Well, I guess I am a little bit nervous," she admitted.

"Why?"

"This is not an orphan baby; this is Carter's baby. He might have certain ways that he wants things done for the baby that are different from what I've always done with the orphan babies. I might not be the kind of mother he wants for Susan."

"Kelli, she is a baby. If you love her, like you love all the babies, everything will be great."

Kelli smiled at the boy. He was so mature for his age; he had such confidence in her. Kelli slipped off the apron that she had been wearing and swiped her hair back, "You're right Charlie. I'll do what I always did at the orphanage. I'm sure that I can take care of one small baby girl, and if Carter wants me to do things differently, he can show me and I will do my best."

Just then the front door creaked opened and they heard Carter enter the house. Kelli and Charlie couldn't hold themselves back any longer. They rushed out into the front room and came to a screeching halt in front of him.

Carter stood in the middle of the room with a bundle in his arms. He was surprised when Kelli and Charlie had come pounding out of the kitchen, but it was nice to see such genuine eagerness on their faces. Carter could tell that they were keen to see the baby, so he lowered his arms and pulled back the edge of the blanket. Kelli stepped closer and looked at the child. Charlie stood on his tip toes, trying to peek over the edge of the blanket.

For Kelli, it was instant love. She could tell that Susan was one of the sweetest babies she had ever seen. A huge grin spread over Charlie's face. He obviously thought she was something special as well.

"May I hold her?" Kelli asked hesitantly. She did not want to push. Carter might need time to learn to trust her with his daughter.

Carter was pleased at Charlie and Kelli's reaction to Susan. He felt no qualms in allowing Kelli to hold Susan. He gently handed the child to her, but stood ready to take her back right away if she showed any signs of fear. Usually, if Susan did not like someone, she would start crying right away.

Carter held his breath, hoping that Susan would like Kelli. He waited, and was relieved that there was no outburst from the small bundle. Carter was amazed that Susan was smiling as Kelli cooed to her.

"Oh, Carter, she is beautiful."

"Just like her mama…" Carter stopped dead, angry at himself for once more dragging Abby's name into the conversation.

Kelli looked up at him, disturbed by his hesitation. "Carter, I know that you loved your first wife, and she was Susan's mother. Susan will want to know all about her. I don't want it to be a secret that Susan always has to wonder about, nor do I want it to be a problem between us. Feel free to talk about her whenever you want to."

"Thank-you, Kelli. This is very difficult for me. I want Susan to have a good mother, and I believe you will be that. I also want Susan to know about Abby."

"Then don't stop yourself from talking about her."

"It's not fair to you though. I agreed to marry you Kelli, but you know as well as I do that it was an arrangement for Susan's sake. I'm just not sure how I feel about having another wife yet. I don't want to hurt you with my memories of Abby."

"I understood the situation before I married you Carter. I won't allow myself to be hurt because you have memories of your first wife. I want to know all about her too. There may be times when Susan asks me about her mother, and I want to have some answers for her."

Carter smiled gratefully.

"Just give God time to work things out between us," Kelli spoke softly. "He knows the plans he has for you and for me as well."

Carter caught himself staring into Kelli's eyes. They were really very beautiful eyes.

"Hey, what about me, I want to see my sister." Charlie was hopping up and down trying to see into the bundle.

"Whoa!" Carter placed his hand on the boy's shoulder to calm him down. "How bout you sit down in a chair and then you can hold her." Carter looked at Kelli for her agreement. She nodded.

"You don't need to worry about Charlie. He has held so many babies at the orphanage. All the little ones just loved him."

Charlie scooted towards the chair by the fire. Kelli walked over and settled the child into the boy's arms. Charlie fell in love at once. He began talking to the baby in a quiet voice.

He told her all about how he had come to Kansas on the Orphan Train, and how Carter had adopted him to be her big brother.

After a few moments, Charlie looked earnestly up at Carter and stated. "I'm going to be the best brother in the whole world."

"I know you will, Son. I know you will." Carter reached over and ruffled the boy's hair.

"I like girl babies best of all," Charlie added. "I'm glad Susan is a girl and not a boy."

Carter gave Charlie a small wink to indicate that he was in agreement with him, but he wondered if he really did agree. Carter had been very happy when the doctor placed the sweet and healthy baby girl in his arms, but he had felt a moment of disappointment as well. He had secretly wished for a son. Abby had made it clear though that this was the only child she was ever willing to have. She did not like what being in the family way because of what it had done to her figure; so Carter had hoped for a boy.

When Susan was born and Abby did not survive, Carter was so glad that the child had lived that it did not matter any longer if she were a boy or not. He was just happy to have his child.

Now he had Charlie as well. Although the young boy was not his own child by birth, Carter already felt the bond that he knew only existed between a father and son. Carter squatted next to him and they took turns cooing to the little girl.

Kelli sat across from them and watched as Carter and Charlie snuggled the baby. She couldn't help but feel a bit envious; not at their attention to the baby, but over the relationship that had already seemed to develop between them.

Carter already acted like a true father to the boy and Charlie was more than eager to behave as a son. Of course, having loved Charlie his whole life, Kelli completely understood how easy it was for Carter to bond with the young boy. She reminded herself that she wanted Charlie to be happy and it was a good thing that Carter seemed to genuinely care for him.

Kelli looked at the baby again. Perhaps she and Susan would have a similar bond in time. Right now Susan was too young to really bond, but it wouldn't be long before she was crawling, then walking and talking. Kelli was sure by then that she and Susan would truly be mother and daughter. She loved Charlie with all her heart, but she had plenty of room for a daughter as well.

After a few moments, Kelli reached out and took the baby into her own arms. It was wonderful to hold a child again. She had not liked life in the orphanage at all but caring for and loving the babies had made it all worth while. Kelli hoped that loving Susan would make this false marriage worthwhile as well.

"Isn't she the sweetest thing?" Charlie asked.

"For a girl she is," Kelli assured him. "But, I remember a little boy who I thought was the sweetest one I ever saw."

Charlie's face lit up and he turned to Carter and proudly announced, "She means me."

Carter laughed. "I'm sure she does. I can just imagine you as a little baby."

Kelli nodded and spoke softly so she wouldn't disturb Susan, who had nodded off in her arms. "He had the longest eyelashes you have ever seen. And he had more hair than most of the girl babies at the orphanage He was a beautiful baby."

"Well, I'd say he is a pretty good looking young man, and he still has plenty of hair." Carter tussled the boy's hair once more.

Charlie tucked his head in embarrassment.

Kelli laughed.

"Cut it out, Kelli." He did not want Kelli to treat him like a baby in front of Carter. "Pa, can I teach Susan to milk the cows?"

Even Kelli laughed at that.

"I think she is a bit young for that, but when she gets older I'm sure you can teach her."

Charlie got up and stood next to Kelli, then he snuggled down in the chair next to her and peeked into the blanket at the baby's cherub face.

"You hear that Susan? Someday I'm going to teach you to milk a cow." The baby gurgled and smiled back at her new big brother.

Charlie turned and whispered into Kelli's ear, "See, Kelli, that's another reason that Carter needs us. To take care of Susan."

Chapter 8

It did not take long for Kelli to adjust to her life in the comfortable new home. She was kept very busy taking care of Susan and Charlie, cooking and cleaning, sewing and washing. All in all it was hard work and there were many things she had to learn, because they were different than in New York, but overall she was extremely content.

In the early mornings, she loved to stand on the front porch of her own little house and look out over the yard and fields, full of ripe wheat, and further on to the untamed fields with their blue hue. This was her quiet time, before the children awoke, before Carter came in for breakfast. This was the time she lifted her prayers of thanksgiving over and over again to God.

Susan was a sweet baby and Charlie was the happiest boy in the world. He loved his job of milking the cow. He woke up early in the mornings, jumped out of bed and rushed out to the barn to make sure that Carter hadn't started the milking. He was determined to do the one thing he was capable of doing to the best of his ability. When he returned to the house each day, carrying the large bucket of cool, fresh milk, his eyes were always lit with pride.

Kelli learned how to churn butter from the milk, although it was a long, tiresome process. She was glad that Charlie helped with that. During the day, Charlie stayed near the house in case Kelli needed help with Susan or other chores. The actual farm work was too difficult for him at this point, due to the brace on his leg, and because he was still rather small and skinny, but he was always happy to help out in anyway he could.

Kelli and Charlie worked in the garden every day. They were pleased when they saw the first small sprouts peeking out from the soil in just a few weeks. Kelli noticed that Charlie was growing stronger daily. His skin glowed from the tan he got from being outside in the sun.

Every chance they could get, both Charlie and Kelli would go swimming. They had promised Carter to never go near the creek alone, so they had to wait for Carter to finish with his chores. As Carter had promised, swimming was beginning to strengthen Charlie's leg, so the boy wanted to swim every day. Some nights though, Carter was too tired for swimming lessons, and they would just rinse off quickly at the side of the creek. Carter had been good to his word, however, remembering to rub Charlie's leg every night with ointment.

Kelli learned to enjoy bathing in the creek, especially since Carter had given her a sweet smelling bar of soap to use. She had also asked Carter to string up a rope near the creek where they could all hang their clothes to dry. Remembering how embarrassed she was on her first bathing adventure, she always remembered to take a proper cover so that when she emerged from the water, she would not be exposed. She was determined that Carter would not be able to see her undergarments ever again, even if the ones she wore now were perfectly new.

Although her days were spent caring for the children, working in the garden, and cooking, she looked forward to the evenings the most. After the final dishes were done, Kelli would gather the clothing that needed mending and she would sit in front of the big fireplace in the living room sewing. Carter would sit opposite her and they would talk. They had settled into a fairly relaxed friendship.

Carter enjoyed being able to tell Kelli about the farm and Kelli loved sharing with him all the events of her day and about the cute things the children did.

One night, while they sat in front of the fire, Carter interrupted Kelli's thoughts.

"I've never asked you when your birthday is."

"No, and I haven't asked you either," Kelli joked.

"I'm serious," Carter insisted. "I need to know when my wife's birthday is so I can get her a gift."

Kelli blushed. "You've already given me so much Carter. You've given me a real home, and a garden and clothes and... well just about everything I've ever prayed for."

Carter was pleased by Kelli's words, but he knew that there was something left out. He was aware that Kelli wanted to have a real marriage and that was the one thing he still did not feel he could give her. Every time he thought he was growing closer to her, thoughts of Abby would slam his heart and mind.

"Well, if you really must know, my birthday is next Sunday."

Carter sat up straight. "What! That soon? You should have told me."

"I really did not think it mattered. It has never been very important."

"Not important? Birthdays are very important."

Kelli couldn't understand why Carter felt so adamant about it.

"At the orphanage if anyone knew their birthday, they kept it to themselves. It was a special secret. They did not allow us to celebrate because there were many children who did not know when their real birthdays were."

Carter sat back again. "No one should have to live that kind of life." His voice turned soft and sympathetic. Kelli had never liked sympathy before, but from Carter it seemed warm and genuine.

"Thank-you for caring, but it was just the way things were. I never felt bad about it. I had my memories of the years I lived with my parents. My mother always made me a cake and my parents always gave me a small gift on my birthday. I was luckier than most of the orphans who never even knew their parents."

"I'll tell you what," Carter suddenly bellowed. "I've wanted to be able to introduce you to our neighbors and to some of the friends I have in town, but I haven't had time. I think I will just host a birthday party for you, right here and invite them all."

Kelli stared at him with a horrified expression on her face.

"You don't like the idea?"

"What if they don't like me?"

"I'm sure that if you are your sweet self, everyone will like you."

"Have you forgotten the way that the general store owner acted? Once everyone knows about me being an orphan they will all treat me the same way that he did." Her shoulders sagged.

"Not everyone is as rude as him. I think the people out here will be kind. You may get a few looks of sympathy, but I do not believe that most of my friends would be outwardly rude."

"They will all make fun of the way I asked you to marry me." Kelli's voice trembled. It had never occurred to her before what impact her impulsive behavior may have on Carter's reputation in the town.

Carter shrugged. "I am not worried about any of that Kelli. There are a few farmers who live near here who married mail order brides."

"But that's just it. I wasn't a mail order bride. We won't even be able to say that, because the general store owner knows that I was on the Orphan Train. He did not look like the type of person to keep that a secret."

Carter chuckled. "That is the truth. I'd say that five minutes after we left his store, he had already told at least ten other people about us."

"You see what I mean? It could be really embarrassing for you Carter. I never wanted to cause that."

Carter reached out and took Kelli's hands in his.

"Kelli, I am not embarrassed about our marriage. I needed a mother for Susan and you needed a home. If anyone has a problem with the choice we made, they don't have to come to the party. I will get a feel for most everyone's opinion when I get to town. I won't invite anyone who I think might have an issue with our relationship. So, have I eased your fears?"

"I wouldn't know what to do, or what to say to anyone," Kelli murmured.

"Kelli, everyone will enjoy meeting you. You are a very pleasant person to talk to and you are interesting as well. I'm sure that it will all turn out great." Carter tried to assure her, but the look on her face indicated her doubt.

"Do we have to have it so soon?" Kelli thought that if she could put it off long enough, Carter would forget the whole thing, but Carter shook his head.

"It is the perfect time. We have to start harvesting the wheat in another week or so and it's always good for everyone's spirits to have a social before the harvest. Instead of holding one in town, we can have it right here, and in your honor. That will give all the farmers and townsfolk an excuse to get together and have some fun before the hard work hits."

There was nothing more Kelli could say in rebuttal. She could tell that Carter had made up his mind about this.

Carter recognized her sigh of acceptance. A grin spread across his face.

"Is there anything special you would like to have?"

"I can't think of a thing."

"Okay little lady, then don't be too shocked if I give you something that you don't want or need."

Kelli struggled with her emotions. She was very unhappy with the idea of the party, and yet, she was excited to think that Carter wanted to buy a gift for her. It had been so long since anyone gave Kelli a gift; she could hardly remember it at all. "I'm serious, Carter. I do not need a thing."

"Kelli, in this house, everyone gets a gift on their birthday." Carter stood and stretched. "It's getting late. I've got to hit the hay."

Kelli smiled up at him, admiring his tall frame, but her eyes still flashed uncertainty about the proposed party. "I'll just finish these last few stitches and I'll head to bed too."

Carter gazed at her for a moment. She seemed exceptionally sweet tonight. It was so unusual to meet a woman who didn't want gifts. Since their marriage, Kelli had not asked for anything and that concerned him. Carter wasn't sure if she was afraid to ask or if she were really just totally content. He couldn't imagine that it was true contentment. Carter knew most of the woman in Emporia, and not one of them was content with what they had.

"Are you afraid to ask me for things?"

Surprise registered in Kelli's eyes. "No, I am not afraid. So far you have provided more than I ever had before in my life. I can't even imagine what else I could need."

"Isn't there anything you just want, even if you don't need it? Most women like hats, ribbons or other frilly things"

"I don't need any of those things, Carter. I have everything I want or need already."

The firelight danced in her eyes, as Kelli assured Carter that she was truly satisfied. Carter felt himself being drawn to her. He stepped closer, gently bent over and pressed a small kiss on her forehead. Kelli sat perfectly still, afraid to move and spoil this special moment.

When he straightened up again, Carter cleared his throat. "Good night then," he said and abruptly walked away.

Kelli finished the row of stitches, dropped the shirt into the basket beside her chair and slipped down onto her knees. She had formed the habit of kneeling beside her small bed each evening, but tonight she felt the need to pray here and now. Her voice was low and sweet.

Oh Lord, I thank-You that Carter seems to really care about me. I'm not too sure about this party he wants to have. I'm afraid that the people will laugh at Carter for marrying me. I don't want to be an embarrassment to him. He is so kind and special.

Kelli sat quietly, letting her heart fill with the presence of God. She reflected on her marriage and then continued her prayer.

Lord, as I've mentioned, I want Carter and I to have a real marriage. I want to be able to fill the empty place he has inside. Help him to see that I am not here to replace Abby or to steal her place in his heart, but help him find room for me in his heart as well. And finally Lord, help me to be brave enough to ask Carter about his faith in you. Amen.

After her short prayer, Kelli felt at peace again. She stood and picked up her basket. With a final glance around the room, she headed back to the kitchen to make sure that everything in there was also put away for the evening. Since her back was turned away from the hallway where the bedrooms were, she had not noticed Carter standing in the shadow. She did not know that he had over heard her earnest, honest prayer.

Carter turned and slipped quietly back to his room, grateful that Kelli hadn't seen him standing in the shadows. After hearing Kelli's heartfelt prayer, he forgot what had taken him out in the hallway to begin with.

Dolefully, Carter sat on the end of the bed for a long time thinking over the words she had spoken. His heart was heavy. It just wasn't right that Kelli had to beg God for a real marriage. Even if they had agreed that this would be a marriage in name only, Carter knew that in God's eyes, the way they were living was wrong. God expected him to treat Kelli as a real wife. It didn't matter if Carter wasn't ready for a new wife, he had taken one, and it was his responsibility to treat her appropriately. Carter ran his hand through his hair and sighed. "How can I fix this?"

Carter slunk off the bed and dropped onto his knees, his head bent in prayer; the first real prayer he had prayed since Abby died.

Lord, forgive me for being angry with You for so long. I know that You didn't take Abby away from me. She just wasn't meant for this kind of life. Lord, thank-You for sending Kelli into my life, to care for Susan and I. Forgive me Father, I know I did the wrong thing by marrying Kelli just so I would have a mother for Susan, I realize now that I was being selfish. I don't want Kelli to be hurt by this any longer. Lord, I want to be a real husband to Kelli and for her to be my real wife, I just don't know what to do. Show me the way Lord, please show me the way.

Carter's cheeks were damp from the tears that had fallen from his eyes during his prayer. He stood and wiped them. He moved quietly around the room, preparing for bed. When he was finally between his sheets, he took a deep relaxing breath. The heaviness he had felt for so long was gone, along with the pain that had held his heart in it's clutches ever since Abby died. He was at peace.

Carter was not exactly certain what he was going to do about his relationship with Kelli, but he was sure of one thing; he was going to do something about it. He was going to make changes, and with continued prayer, he was confident that God would show him how to make the right adjustments. Thoughts and plans ran through his mind until sleep finally overtook him.

When the sun was barely up, Carter stirred and opened his eyes. He lay still for a moment, then slipped off the bed onto his knees. The first change he was going to make was to start each day in prayer. He spent a few minutes thanking God for his life, his children and his new wife.

After his prayer time Carter eagerly dressed. He was excited to begin his new life, but he realized that he must hold himself back.

He couldn't just rush up to Kelli and declare that he was ready for them to be a real husband and wife. It did not matter that Kelli had prayed for that. Carter believed that Kelli deserved to be courted. Regardless of the fact that they were already married, Carter determined to begin all over again and to treat her as if they had only just met. He vowed to show her that he was interested in getting to know her better, in sharing not only his house with her, but his heart as well.

Carter stood looking in the small mirror that hung on the wall over his chest of drawers. He wondered if Kelli found him appealing at all. She wanted a real marriage, but that didn't tell how she felt about him. Carter knew he was a handsome man, and he had always been a favorite with women, but then again, women could be kind of fickle. He only hoped that Kelli liked his looks.

Well, she is married to me, so I guess she's stuck with me no matter what. I'll have to win her heart with my actions.

Carter tried to remember how he had acted when he was courting Abby, but he quickly brushed those thoughts aside. Kelli was completely different than Abby and he needed to treat her in ways that would make her feel special. He was so intent on his thoughts, that it never occurred to him that the thoughts of Abby had not hurt.

When Carter finally stepped out of his room he could smell the mouth watering aroma of flap jacks. Kelli was in the kitchen cooking. Carter grinned. This was one of the things he liked the most about Kelli; she could cook. He stepped into the kitchen rubbing his stomach.

"Something sure smells good in here."

Kelli turned a bit startled. She was surprised to see the smile on his face. He wasn't usually so cordial in the mornings, but then she recalled the kiss he had bestowed on her forehead the evening before. Kelli's cheeks turned pink at the memory. Kelli ducked her head and hoped that Carter did not notice her discomfort.

Don't make a big deal of it, she thought. *It probably didn't mean anything. He was just being nice, because I was talking about being an orphan. It was just a sympathetic kiss, that's all.*

"Good morning, Carter." Kelli's voice was soft and a bit unsure. "Sit down, I'm cooking flap jacks." She pointed to the chair.

Carter rubbed his hands together. "Yummy, one of my favorites," he joked, as he pulled out the chair and sat. His eyes never left her face. "You are a very good cook, Kelli."

Kelli was pleased by his compliment. Learning to cook over the fire had been challenging for her, but she had adapted well. Her face flushed from the flattering remark

"Thank-you. I enjoy cooking."

Carter turned around and looked at the fireplace and winced. "I almost hate to get you a stove, since you've learned to cook over the fire so well, but I do think I will order one. Would you like that?"

"That's too expensive, Carter. I don't need one. I'm learning the tricks of cooking over the fire."

Kelli swished passed Carter as she set the platter of flap jacks on the table. Carter reached out and grabbed her hand. He held it gently in his and patted it. "I can afford a stove Kelli. I want to make it easy on you if I can. Maybe that could be your birthday present."

Kelli swallowed. She wasn't sure what to say to him. She noted that just standing close to Carter made it hard for her to breath. She was very attracted to this golden man.

A strange grin was splashed across his face and his eyes bore straight into hers. Kelli could not even begin to imagine what had come over him. First he had kissed her last night, and now he was telling her that he wanted to make things easy for her. Kelli felt as if her world was somehow spinning too fast for her. She wasn't sure how to react to his strange behavior. Did his actions somehow mean that his feelings were changing; that he was starting to fall in love with her? Kelli's heart pounded with excitement at the thought.

The moment was interrupted by Charlie, as he entered the kitchen, carrying his pail of milk. "Whatcha doing, Pa?"

Charlie set the pail on the shelf. He didn't notice the strain between Carter and Kelli. "We gonna eat now, Kelli?"

Carter dropped Kelli's hand reluctantly, and turned to face the boy. He wore a welcoming smile for Charlie, even though the boy had unknowingly interrupted what could have turned into a special moment for Kelli and himself.

Kelli turned back to cooking, slightly disappointed that the moment had been lost. She thought that Carter had been about to tell her something important.

Charlie sidled up to the table and sat down. The room was silent. The boy looked from Kelli back to Carter, trying to work out what was going on between them. He sat quietly, waiting for his food. Usually they all talked and laughed during their meals, but today there was something wrong. "Daisy acted kind of funny today, Pa."

Carter's head lifted. "What do you mean?"

"She wasn't as easy to milk as usual. She pushed me away a few times, and when I finally got the milk to come out, it was slow."

"Hmmm, I better have the doctor come out to see her." He leaned over and patted Charlie's shoulder. "You know Charlie, Daisy is pretty old."

Charlie did not even want to think about what that meant. Instead he changed the conversation. "You gonna work in the fields today, Pa?"

"Not today. I'm going to town to invite all my friends here for Kelli's birthday party. Would you like to come along with me?"

Kelli turned with a surprised expression. She was sure that he would have changed his mind about the party once he had time to think it over. She did not say anything, however. If he was determined to have a party for her, the least she could do was appreciate it.

"A party!" Charlie shouted. "Did you hear that Kelli? You're going to have a birthday party." A grin spread across the young boy's face.

Charlie had never experienced a birthday party before, because he had been raised in the orphanage, but a few of the other children who came to live at the orphanage when they were seven years old or older had told him all about the birthday parties they had enjoyed before they were left at the orphanage. Charlie had sometimes doubted the stories he was told, but he hoped that Kelli's party would include a cake and presents.

"Yes, I heard, Charlie. I have tried to explain to Carter that I do not need to have a birthday party, but he is determined."

The boy searched Kelli's face. If she were truly against the party, he would stand firm with her. No matter how much he loved Carter, if it came to making a decision between what Carter wanted or what Kelli wanted, Kelli was and always would be his first choice.

"If Kelli doesn't want a party, then I don't want to go to town with you," he explained to Carter reluctantly. He was disappointed but unwilling to go against Kelli's wishes.

Carter smiled at the boy. "If Kelli really doesn't want a party, I suppose we could just have a quiet celebration here; just the four of us."

Charlie turned and looked at Kelli. His eyes appealing to her softer side. "Even if you don't need a party, it would still be nice to have one, wouldn't it, Kelli?"

Kelli could see that the boy was willing to stand up for her decision, even if it meant missing out on something that he would love to participate in. She walked over and hugged him. She realized that it would be unfair for her to deny Charlie this experience. Charlie would enjoy the party even if she didn't.

"Yes, I think it would be nice to have a party, Charlie, so why don't you go with Carter to town and help him?"

Charlie's face exploded with excitement.

Carter turned to Kelli. "Are you sure?"

Kelli nodded.

"Would you like to go to town? There must be some things you need. You can shop while Charlie and I visit all my friends."

Charlie was rocking back and forth excitedly. "Sure, Kelli, you come with us."

Kelli could not think of a single thing that she needed for herself or for Charlie. There were a few items that she could use in the kitchen, but the idea of facing the general store owner again this soon, was too much for her to bear.

"Could I just give you a list?" she asked Carter. "I want to work in the garden today."

Carter did not like the idea of leaving Kelli alone. He had never left Abby on the farm alone. She always wanted to go to town with him.

Kelli could see the hesitation on his face. "I'll be fine here Carter. I'm not afraid of being left alone."

He was amazed that she was able to read his thoughts so easily.

"Okay, Kelli, but I might stop at a neighbor's house on the way out, and ask if she'll drive over and visit with you." Carter saw the look of disapproval flash onto Kelli's face. "I would feel a lot better if I knew that you were not completely alone for the whole day."

Kelli was not used to someone worrying about her, and even though she wasn't interested in meeting any of his neighbors, she could tell that Carter was just doing what he thought best. She nodded her head in agreement, although she could already feel her palms starting to sweat with nervousness. She had no idea how to treat a neighbor. Should she serve tea and scones? Kelli began to search through the kitchen supplies to see if she had everything she would need to make scones.

Charlie was hopping up and down with excitement. He hoped to get another piece of candy from the store if Carter offered. Of course, he would never ask for one. Kelli had explained that Carter was a kind and generous man, but that they should never take advantage of that.

"We need to be happy and content with anything that Carter chose to give us, and never to ask for anything more," Kelli told Charlie.

"Sit back down and finish your meal," Carter insisted.

Charlie could barely swallow the food. When they finished, Carter asked Kelli if she needed help cleaning up. She shook her head and insisted they get started.

Carter and Charlie went out to hitch up the wagon. Kelli cleaned up the dishes and began making a batch of dough for scones. She had decided that scones would be a fine thing to offer the neighbor and if Carter were unable to convince the neighbor to come visit Kelli today, the scones would still be good for breakfast tomorrow

Kelli heard Carter slap the horses with the reins, and then the wheels creaked as the wagon carried Carter and Charlie away from the house. Kelli worked feverishly in the kitchen and in the larger front room, straightening and dusting. She wanted the whole house to shine if a neighbor was going to come by. Once she finished the cleaning, Kelli placed the lovely scones on a plate and covered them with a piece of cheese cloth. Just then she heard the soft mewing sounds of the baby waking up. She slipped into the bedroom and lifted the little girl out of the cradle. Susan's eyes lit up and a smile splashed across her face. It hadn't taken very long for Susan to fall in love with Kelli and for Kelli to fall in love with Susan. Kelli squeezed the child in a hug and the little girl gurgled with baby laughter.

"Well, little one, we are going to have a tea party today, so let's find you a nice dress to wear." Kelli spoke gently as she changed the baby's diaper, washed her and dressed her in a sweet gown. Susan was never fussy and did not make it difficult for Kelli to dress her.

"Now, it's time for me to get cleaned up too." Kelli placed Susan on the floor in the bedroom with a few toys that Carter had carved. Kelli had already filled the basin in her room with warm water. She scrubbed all over until her skin was pink. She remembered the first day of her marriage, when Carter had given the impression that she stunk. She recalled her fear of the creek and the idea of swimming.

Now she wished she had time to go for a full bath in the creek, but she knew that Carter would be mad if he found out that she had gone alone.

"I guess I'm clean enough," she told Susan. Kelli thought about wearing her wool skirt and button up shirt that had been her outfit on the Orphan Train. They were made of good sturdy quality material and made her look mature, but her mind rebuked the idea of the hot clothes. She finally just slipped a clean calico dress on over her head. Kelli stood before the mirror and scrutinized herself. She wondered what the neighbor would think of her.

"I am who I am," she finally proclaimed and turned away from her reflection.

Kelli carried the baby out to the kitchen and placed her inside the wooden box that Carter had put in the kitchen. It was a safe place where Susan could play while Kelli cooked. Kelli set the water near the fire, ready to bring it to a boil. She set the table with cups, saucers and plates. She used a beautiful Blue Willow set that Abby had owned. Kelli touched each item lovingly. They brought back a flicker of a long ago memory.

*I think that my mother used to own dishes with the same pattern. T*he thought brought a rush of warmth into Kelli's heart. It was so nice to actually be able to remember anything about her life before the orphanage.

When everything was ready for the potential guest's visit, Kelli carried Susan onto the front porch. She sat on the wicker chair and began to sing to Susan. The baby relaxed in Kelli's arms and quietly sucked her thumb. Kelli wasn't sure just how long it would be, if at all, before the neighbor would arrive, but she was as ready as she would ever be.

Chapter 9

It wasn't long before Kelli saw a wagon in the distance, headed towards her. She could tell that it was one lone driver; a woman. Kelli gulped in some air, realizing that she had been holding her breath. She set Susan down on a blanket beside the rocking chair. Susan was content to sit. As the wagon drew nearer, Kelli stood and wiped the wrinkles off her dress.

The woman on the wagon waved in a friendly fashion, which helped to ease some of Kelli's worry.

When the woman called out, "Whoa!" to the horses, Kelli stepped down from the front porch and approached the side of the buckboard.

"Hello, hello!" The woman called down in an exuberant voice. "You must be Kelli."

"Yes, I am," Kelli watched as the woman clambered down from the wagon. In just a second the woman was standing in front of her, and to Kelli's embarrassment, the woman boldly and openly looked her up and down.

"You're a might thin." The words came out like a snort.

Kelli wasn't really sure how to respond to that. She felt as if she had already been found lacking.

"You sure you're strong enough to live on the prairie?"

Kelli's heart filled with dismay. It was obvious this woman had only come to inspect Kelli, not befriend her. A sharp retort welled up, but Kelli pushed it down, remembering she was a Christian and needed to act like one. This was Carter's neighbor, so she must be kind and try to get along.

"I'm sorry, but Carter did not tell me your name."

The woman turned with an astonished look on her face. "Well, that sure does surprise me. I've been helping Carter care for little Susan for so long. Carter always relies on me to help. I'm sure that is why he asked me to come out here today."

Kelli just stared at the woman. She kept trying to think of a way to respond to the woman's comment.

The woman fidgeted with her dress and bonnet. Her eyes almost dared Kelli to contradict anything she said. Finally she huffed, "Oh, I'm Lila Aderson. I am your closest neighbor."

"It's nice to meet you Mrs. Aderson."

"It's just Miss!" the woman corrected

"Miss Aderson. I appreciate you coming over to visit. How far is it to your home?"

"Not far at all. That is why it was so convenient for Carter and me to... I mean for Carter to bring Susan to me."

Kelli didn't miss the slip. She had never met anyone quite like Lila Aderson, but she could tell that the woman was up to no good. It was obvious that she had meant to imply that there was some kind of relationship that existed between Carter and herself.

Kelli stepped back, wondering exactly what benefit the woman thought she would get by this strategy. Kelli never thought for a moment that Carter was interested in Lila. He was still in love with Abby.

Both women stood staring at one another. Neither ready to back down.

This is not the way to treat my neighbor, Kelli thought. She dropped her eyes and took a small step backwards.

"I have tea and scones ready. Won't you step inside?"

"Why sure, honey. Of course, I've been here so many times, it's like a second home to me." She flounced up the steps, passed Susan without even acknowledging the baby, and boldly pushed open the front door.

Kelli bent over and gently picked up the baby. When she straightened up, she shook her head in wonder and followed Lila into the house.

Lila stood in the middle of the great room; her eyes scanning everything. Kelli thought that it seemed like the woman was searching the room for something.

"Haven't changed much have you? Course I can't blame you. I'm sure Carter insisted on keeping all of his wife's things just where she had them. He loved that woman so much."

Kelli could tell by the tone of voice that Lila was still trying to be cruel. She couldn't understand just why. Somehow the woman had taken offense to Kelli's presence here. Kelli wanted to say something pleasant, but in her own defense she murmured, "As a matter of fact, my husband suggested I get rid of anything I didn't like. I have chosen to keep most of the lovely things that Abby had here so that Susan can grow up with them as part of her life. It is only fair that she have the lovely things that belonged to her mother, don't you agree?"

"Humph! I suppose that's the right thing. I just think it would bother you to have all of Carter's first wife's things out in plain sight, reminding him of his first love."

Kelli flushed at this statement. She tried to brush off the comment, but it cut into her soul. Somehow, this woman was able to make her feel insignificant.

Suddenly, Lila walked over and scooped Susan out of Kelli's arms. "Ain't she the sweetest thing? I spent so much time with her that I thought she was gonna start calling me Mama."

Susan whimpered and grew stiff in Lila's arms.

Kelli did not like to see the way that Lila held Susan. It did not look as if she had ever held a baby before at all. Kelli wondered if Lila had really taken time to hold Susan before. Kelli tried to imagine Lila doting on the child, but could not conjure up the image. She wondered how Lila had treated Susan all the times she had watched her.

"Why don't I just take Susan and put her down for a nap while you and I have tea?" Kelli wanted to sweep the baby away from the offending woman's arms.

Lila shoved Susan back into Kelli's embrace. "That's a good idea." Lila wiped her hands on her skirt as if holding the child had made them dirty somehow. Kelli cringed when she thought about this woman taking care of Susan.

Couldn't Carter tell that Lila didn't really like Susan?

Kelli took Susan to the room they shared, and placed her in the cradle beside the bed. She rocked the cradle a few moments and Susan started to drift off to sleep. Before Kelli could step back out of the room, Lila stepped in.

"Oh, my! Isn't this quaint." She smirked as she looked around the room and noted Kelli's personal items set out on the dresser. "You sleep right in here with the baby."

Kelli's cheeks flushed pink. She did not want Lila to know that she slept in here with Susan and not in her husband's room. Kelli wasn't about to allow this woman to embarrass her, or to leave the house with that type of gossip.

"Oh, I just put my things in here because Carter's room, I mean our room, was already decorated so handsomely. Some nights, if Susan is restless, I just slip in here and lay down on the bed and sing her to sleep."

The look that crossed Lila's face was one of disbelief. Kelli was content that she had placed a question about it in the woman's mind. Hopefully Lila would not go spread gossip about something she wasn't sure was true or not.

I'm sorry for telling a lie Lord, but what else could I do?

"Now, why don't we go to the kitchen and have our tea?" Kelli herded Lila out of the small room and shut the door behind them. The door to the other room at the end of the hall was open.

"Oh, that's right," Lila sneered. "I heard that Carter had actually adopted an orphan boy. Is that his room now?" She pointed at the open door.

"Yes."

"I was so shocked to hear about the boy. I just saw the boy when Carter stopped to ask me to come over and visit with you. I had heard he was a cripple. I did not think that Carter would take the risk of bringing a strange boy into the house around Susan. He has always been so protective of her."

Kelli was nearly ready to slap the woman's face. Luckily she was behind Lila when the woman spoke the hateful words.

"Charlie adores Susan and dotes on her all the time. Carter feels very comfortable allowing Susan to be held by his new son."

"Charlie? Is that the orphan's name?"

"Yes, his name is Charlie, but he is no longer an orphan. He is Carter's son."

The woman smirked.

When they reached the kitchen, Kelli offered Lila a chair.

Lila sat at the table and Kelli brought the plate of scones over, set them on the table and then began to pour the tea. Lila was silent, watching Kelli's movements around the kitchen.

"Did you have any trouble finding your way around in here?"

Kelli's face showed her perplexed thoughts. "Not at all, why?"

"Last time I was here, I peeked into several cupboards and thought it was all a jumble. There were so many things I would have changed to make it more convenient."

"I didn't need to move anything," Kelli assured her. "Carter's first wife had everything in places that are very suitable." Kelli could hardly believe that she was defending Abby. "Do you take cream and sugar?"

"Just cream."

Kelli handed her the small pitcher of cream and then she sat down across from the woman. She slowly sipped her own tea.

"It was nice of Carter to stop by today and ask me to come over and sit with you a spell. I'm so surprised about Carter getting married, and even more surprised about him adopting such a young child. Carter needs a helper, that's for sure, but I don't see what a small boy like that can do. Where did he come from?"

When Lila lifted her cup and took a sip, Kelli spoke.

"The boy that Carter adopted came from New York on the Orphan Train with me. I am an orphan also." Kelli noted the woman raise her eye brows in shock. Obviously the news that Kelli was an orphan had not been spread around yet.

"When Carter and I decided to get married, he was kind enough to adopt Charlie as well." Kelli wished that Lila would leave. This was not turning out to be a very pleasant visit. She felt that she needed to stick up for Charlie in some way.

"By the way," she stated. "Charlie does all the milking now, and that is where we get that lovely cream you are using in your tea." Kelli spoke this in retaliation to Lila's rude comments earlier.

For a moment, Lila sat quietly staring at the younger woman. Kelli glared back. They seemed to have reached an impasse. Finally Lila shrugged.

"I'm sorry, Kelli," Lila spoke contritely. Kelli's eyes shot up in surprise. "I've been saying such awful things to you ever since I got here and you don't deserve any of them."

Kelli wasn't sure how to respond, so she remained silent.

"It's just that when I heard that Carter had gotten married, I was so angry and full of jealously. I've been taking care of Susan for him, even though I don't really like children very much, because I had hoped that Carter would marry me."

Kelli tried to imagine Carter and Lila married, but was unable to even fathom Carter and this cold, irritating woman together.

"He was never interested in me."

Lila set her cup down, reached into her dress pocket and pulled out a handkerchief. She dabbed her eyes and Kelli could see that real tears hovered in the older woman's eyes.

Kelli reached out to pat the woman's hand.

"I was only kidding myself. I've known since the first time that Carter asked for my help that he wasn't ever going to ask me to marry him."

"Do you love him?" Kelli asked, even though she wasn't sure she really wanted to know the answer to that question. She always thought that it was rather rude of her to ask such a personal thing, but Lila didn't seem insulted at all.

"At first I thought I did. I was attracted to him. But after a while, I knew that I did not love him. I just want to get married and Carter is a good man. I'm thirty five years old and haven't found anyone yet. I hate the idea that I will never get married."

"I'm sorry. Aren't there any men in town who you might be interested in?"

Lila took another sip of her tea and a small giggle escaped her lips. It reminded Kelli of a school girl, although it sounded awkward coming from Lila.

"Yes, I do like Doctor Martin, but it seemed more convenient to be interested in Carter since we lived so close. I've really wasted my time though and now I've come over here and made a fool of myself."

Kelli wasn't sure she believed the woman's repentant words, but she wanted to give her a chance. After all, Lila couldn't hurt them now that she and Carter were married.

"I think we should start all over again," Kelli suggested.

"I would like that very much. And to be honest with you, I've only been in this house once or twice. I only said those things about the kitchen out of pure orneriness."

Kelli smiled. There was nothing to say to that. She was glad that Lila was able to admit her own faults though.

Lila blew her nose into her hanky. "These are lovely scones. Will you give me the recipe?"

"Of course. I wasn't sure if they would turn out since cooking over an open fire is so new to me."

"Well, they are just wonderful. Maybe I could make them and serve them when I invite Doctor Martin over for tea next week."

"I think that is a perfect idea. I'll just jot it down on the extra recipe card I have over here." Kelli walked over, got the recipe card and returned to the table. She wrote the short recipe out and handed the card to Lila.

Lila took the card and put away her hanky.

"Now, tell me all about yourself, Kelli. I am just dying to know how you and Carter met."

Kelli knew that people would ask about this and she wasn't completely prepared to answer. She wasn't sure if Carter wanted anyone to know that he had been looking for a mail order bride, or that she had basically thrown herself at him. She took another sip of tea and tried to think of just the right words that would satisfy the question, without causing damage.

"We met in town," Kelli explained. "It all happened so fast, it's still hard for me to grasp it."

"Oh, it must have been love at first sight." The older woman sighed. "I've always dreamed about experiencing it."

Kelli did not interject with any further information. It would be better for Lila to spread the story that she and Carter had fallen madly in love, rather than the story that he was looking for a mail order bride and she offered to fill the position.

Kelli saw Lila watching her. "You do love him, don't you Kelli?"

Kelli bent her head for a moment and allowed the thoughts of Carter to flash through her mind. When she lifted her head, she was prepared to answer truthfully.

"Yes, Lila, I do love Carter."

Chapter 10

The rest of Lila's visit was pleasant. When she left, Kelli wasn't sure if she and the woman could ever be very good friends, but at least she knew that there was someone close by she could go to if she really needed. Kelli stood on the porch waving as Lila drove her wagon away.

Kelli returned to the kitchen and began washing the tea cups and putting away the butter. She reviewed the unique visit, and once again allowed thoughts to flit through her mind. She ran through the conversation she had with Lila over and over again, wondering if anything she said would reflect badly on Carter. Each time the picture ended with her answering the main question that Lila had asked.

Yes, I do love Carter.

Kelli wasn't sure when it had happened, but she was truly and deeply in love with Carter. Her soul ached for him to feel the same way, but doubted that it would happen. Carter was kind to her and lately he behaved like a man interested in a woman. Perhaps there was some hope after all. For the rest of the afternoon Kelli kept lifting up prayers, asking God to work out the relationship between Carter and herself. She tried to think of ways to make Carter love her.

If it's God's will, He will have to do the work. Kelli reconciled.

It was several hours before Carter and Charlie returned from town. The long trip had curbed some of Charlie's enthusiasm and as soon as the wagon was put away and the horses fed, Charlie ran in the house, gave Kelli a big hug and then rushed to his room to take a small afternoon nap.

Carter had assured him that many men took small rests in the afternoon so that they had the energy to work until the evening. They called it a Siesta.

Kelli set the table quickly, and when Carter stepped in the kitchen she told him to go ahead and sit down. "I've got some scones left and I'm warming up the coffee now."

Carter sat and watched as Kelli slipped around the kitchen. It was amazing how natural she looked. Unlike Abby, Kelli seemed to fit in this house, and she was thriving since coming to live here. He could see that she was no longer as pale and thin as she was when they first met. Good food and sunshine had made some dramatic changes in her; beautiful ones.

When Kelli set the coffee down in front of him, she noticed that he was staring at her. She unconsciously wiped at her face. "Do I have something on my face?"

"No, why?'

"I just thought you were staring at me kind of funny. Sometimes, when a person has something on their face, the other person doesn't know if they should speak up and tell them or not, so they end up just staring at them."

Carter laughed. "Nope, sorry, nothing on your face."

"Good." Kelli sat down beside him and watched as he ate his scone and drank his coffee. Even though he didn't speak, sitting here with Carter was much more pleasant than sitting here with Lila had been.

"Did Lila stop by?" Carter asked.

"Yes."

"Just yes?" Carter's face registered concern. "Did you get along?"

"Not at first, but by the end of the visit we had made a truce."

"A truce? Why?" Carter seemed concerned.

Kelli was shocked. Could it be that Carter seriously did not know what Lila had been thinking all the months she had been caring for Susan? For a moment she was tempted to tell Carter all about the neighbor's visit, but the spirit in her seemed to rebel against that. Finally she decided that Carter would probably only be embarrassed to know about Lila's thoughts and feelings.

"Oh, I think she was just a bit jealous of me living in this gorgeous house," Kelli finally explained. Carter looked around and nodded.

"Well, it is nicer than her house. She still lives in the same house her parents raised her in. They both passed away over the last few years. I'm sorry if you didn't get along with her Kelli. I won't ever send her over here again if you don't like her."

"It's nothing like that. I think she and I will be able to rub along fairly well as neighbors, and even as friends; just not very close friends."

"She seemed eager to meet you," Carter mused. He just could not understand women at all. Lila had never seemed jealous of his house before.

Kelli bit her lip. She did not want to lie to Carter, but the conversation she had with Lila was not something she wanted to share with him.

If Lila told other people that Kelli loved Carter, it would only make sense, since they were married, but Kelli wasn't about to tell Carter that she admitted to Lila that she loved him.

Carter could tell that Kelli was not interested in talking about Lila. It was obvious something had happened she didn't want him to know about. Carter finished his coffee, set down the cup, and decided to change the subject.

"Now, about that birthday party."

"You aren't still serious about that?" Kelli's eyes sparkled with excitement, although she assured Carter that she did not need a party.

"Next week we begin to harvest the wheat. It will require many long hours of hard work for the men and women in this area. I think that all the neighbors will enjoy a party before plunging into the hardest work of the year. Your birthday is a good enough reason for a real shindig. Everyone I spoke to has already agreed to attend. Everyone is anxious to meet you."

What if all the other woman are like Lila? Dread surfaced again.

Carter could easily read the emotions that flit across his wife's face. "Kelli, everyone is eager to meet you. It will be a fine party. You are going to have a wonderful time."

"And who is going to cook for all these people?" Kelli asked. Carter sat dumbfounded. He hadn't even thought about that when he invited everyone.

Kelli giggled. "I guess I can cook for my own party."

"No, I'll pass along the word that everyone should bring something. You can just make one dish and everyone else will make a dish. We can clear out an area in front of the house and set up a table for the food. Everyone can just eat picnic style."

"All right, Carter. It does sound nice."

Inside, Kelli wondered if everyone would treat her the way that the general store owner had, or the way that Lila had. She was sure that there must be a few more women around who had their hopes set on Carter. Carter noticed the look on her face.

"What's worrying you?"

"To be truthful, I'm worried that most of the neighbors will treat me the way that the general store owner did; especially once they know I was an orphan. For some reason people think being an orphan makes you bad."

"I don't think it will be like that. You have to remember that many of the farmers around here come from other countries, so in a way they are orphans too. Just keep your chin up and show them what a beautiful woman you are."

He thinks I'm beautiful, Kelli's heart pounded. "Thank-you, Carter, I will." A slight flush reddened her cheeks.

Carter could tell that the comment about her being beautiful had delighted her. He liked the way her eyes lit up when he gave her the compliment. He decided that he would do that more often. There were many things about Kelli he could compliment.

Don't rush things though, he told himself. *Give her time to trust you.*

Kelli was rather shocked by the words Carter had said to her, but pleased at the same time. She could not understand what had sparked the kind words though, since she was dressed the same way she always dressed, and had her hair in the same braid she always wore.

Carter could see the slight look of embarrassment cross Kelli's face. He did not want to push Kelli away by making her feel self conscious with his comments, so he thought it would be best to leave her alone. He was happy that she seemed genuinely thrilled with the compliment and he planned on giving her many more in the future. But for now, he did not know exactly what to do so he jumped up abruptly.

"Guess, I'll get back to work. If you need any help planning for the picnic, just let me know."

She nodded her head to acknowledge his words. She was afraid to speak out loud and risk him hearing the tremble in her voice. By the strange change of attitude that came over him, Kelli could only guess that he regretted telling her she was beautiful. Her spirit sank. For just a moment she had begun to hope that Carter's heart was softening towards her; that perhaps he did find her attractive.

When Carter was gone, Kelli sat down at the table and slipped her hands together prayerfully. She spent almost an hour pouring out her heart and soul to God. She told Him how hard it was to live with Carter, loving him but not being loved back. She asked God to change her and make her the type of woman Carter would really think was beautiful; a woman who could capture his heart.

When her tears were spent, she slipped into her room and settled onto the small bed next to Susan. In a few moments she fell into an exhausted sleep. The house grew quiet and the sun started to set; Charlie, Susan and Kelli all slept.

When Carter came in for the evening he was caught off guard by the unusual stillness of the room. At first he thought that Kelli and the children must have gone for a walk to the creek, but Kelli had promised not to do that close to dark.

He walked to the door and looked out at the garden, expecting to see Kelli weeding the small plot while Charlie and Susan played nearby, but there was no one in the yard or the garden. Carter walked back into the kitchen and stood in the middle of the room. He listened for the sound of their voices. He heard nothing.

Where are they? he wondered.

As Carter glanced around, he noticed that there was no dinner cooking and the table had not been set for the evening meal. His heart started pounding in anxiety, as he wondered what could have happened to his family.

Carter hurried out of the kitchen and down the hall. He stopped short of rushing into Kelli's room when he saw her asleep on the bed. Her dress was a bit disheveled from sleeping in it. Her hair had slipped loose and lay gently beside her face. Carter stepped closer. He could see traces of dried tear streaks on her cheeks.

There was no doubt in his mind that he had caused those tears with his strange behavior earlier. First giving her a compliment, and then walking out of the house like a distant stranger. She must have been very hurt.

Since Carter had come to terms with his feelings for Kelli, he did not want to cause her pain any longer. He wasn't sure exactly how to act towards her, however.

She was his wife and even if it was only in name, he owed her the respect and honor of treating her decently. There was nothing wrong with telling her she was beautiful; it was a fact. What had been wrong, was the way he had acted afterward; jumping up and leaving the room so quickly.

Carter wondered what she must have thought. He was bereft to see the dried tear streaks on Kelli's lovely cheeks. It had been his plan to begin to court her properly, but it was obvious that his first attempt had been a failure.

Lord, I am going to need Your help with this courtship.

Just then Susan started to sniffle. The soft sound woke Kelli. She sat up startled, wondering at first where she was. Carter barely had time to slip out of the room before Kelli turned towards the door.

Kelli stood up, tried to smooth the wrinkles out of her dress, and then bent over, cooing to the baby girl. "Here you go, Susan," she said reaching down for the child. "Come along, we need to hurry. I overslept and now supper will be late."

Kelli changed the baby out of her wet things into clean, dry clothes. Even though she was in a hurry to get the meal started, she still took the time to cuddle Susan. The little girl squealed with joy.

Carter had rushed into his own room when he noted that Kelli was beginning to stir. He stood in the room holding his breath, hoping that Kelli hadn't noticed him hovering over her bed.

I feel like a young school boy.

Carter heard Susan's happy peals and smiled to himself. He could picture Kelli lifting the child and cuddling her. The image in his mind was very pleasant. It reminded him again that Kelli had kept her part of their wedding bargain. She had taken care of the children, done the cooking and the sewing, and so far had asked for little or nothing in return. Unfortunately, that was also what Carter had given her.

New determination to treat Kelli appropriately and show her that he wanted their's to be a real marriage, filled him. Carter stomped out of his room, down the hall and into the large room. He sat in his chair, pulled the Bible onto his lap and began to read.

Show me what to do Lord, he prayed.

Kelli was surprised to see Carter when she entered the room carrying the baby.

"Oh!" she said in a startled voice. "I did not know you were in the house."

"Everyone was sleeping when I got in."

"I'm sorry that dinner is late. I really don't have any excuse."

Carter looked up at her, and Kelli melted at the sight of his eyes shining in such a friendly manner.

"Kelli, you are my wife, not my servant. You don't have to serve a meal at a certain time. I can totally understand that other things come up from time to time."

"Well, I like to serve the meals around the same time each day. It helps me to keep the children regimented."

Regimentation was the one thing that she had learned living at the orphanage. The whole place had run on rigid rules and timing. It was difficult for Kelli to change her ways now. She was upset that the schedule had been interrupted by a silly cry. Berating herself, Kelli made her way to the kitchen and within a half hour had a nice dinner ready.

Carter was quiet during the meal, but enjoyed every bite. Afterward, he asked Charlie to go out and check on Daisy again.

When Charlie left, Carter told Kelli he wanted to talk to her about the upcoming harvest. "It will take a lot of long hours and hard work. I probably won't be around the house very much."

"Is there anything special that I need to do?"

"Yes, there will be plenty of work. One of the main things I wanted to discuss with you is Charlie. I need you to make sure that he stays close to the house. I know he wants to help, but I just don't think he is strong enough yet. Next year he will be ready."

Charlie would be disappointed, but if Carter said he wasn't ready yet, then Kelli knew it was true. "Do you really think he will be ready by next year?"

"Yes, I can tell he is getting strong. Even his leg seems better. I was thinking that we might want to start taking the brace off his leg and have him spend a bit of time each day without it. I thought I could make him a small crutch to lean on at first."

"Oh, Carter, that is so wonderful. I don't know how to thank you for everything you have done for Charlie."

Carter stared at Kelli for a moment, as the fire light flickered across her face. He found himself mesmerized by her beauty.

"I could think of a few things," he whispered. Kelli noted the look in his eyes and her heart began to pound.

"Anything, Carter," her voice squeaked out.

Suddenly Carter realized what thoughts were flashing through his mind. Guilt for being unfaithful to his first wife surfaced again. He grew agitated. There was a part of him that knew it wasn't wrong to have these feelings for Kelli; she was his wife now and Abby was gone. Yet, at the same time, he still felt as if he were being disloyal to her.

"Uh, well, I guess you could bake me one of your wonderful pies."

Kelli's smile faded. She had hoped that Carter was trying to indicate that he was ready to make her his wife, for real. They had been living together as a married couple for several weeks now, but Carter had made no gesture towards her to indicate that he wanted anything more than a nurse maid for the baby, a housekeeper, a cook and a friend.

A tinge of resentment tried to rear itself up in her spirit, but Kelli quickly extinguished it with a silent prayer.

Lord, help me be patient. I know You have me where You want me to be and I know You have a wonderful life planned for me.

"Yes, Carter. I will make you a pie," she answered quietly, once again reminding herself that she needed to allow Carter time to go through the grieving process for his wife.

Carter stood up facing the fire. Kelli could see the muscles in his back tensing. When he turned back around she noted the serious look on his face.

"Kelli, I think that you have proven to be a wonderful mother to Susan so far. You are a great cook and seem to fit right in here, but..."

Kelli nodded her head in understanding. She wasn't Carter's first wife, and in some ways she was not a wife at all. She was not a woman that Carter had picked himself. She was someone who filled a position that needed to be filled.

Carter said good night and walked away, leaving her alone. A tear slipped down her cheek as it often did in the evenings. Kelli slipped off the chair and got onto her knees.

Lord, you know what it will take to make this a real marriage. I put it in Your hands and ask that you help Carter's heart to heal, so that he could love me.

When she stood up, Kelli noticed the Bible on the stand next to Carter's chair. She still had not gotten up the nerve to talk to him about his faith. That was still a burden on her heart. Even if Carter decided to finally make this a real marriage, Kelli needed to know if she was unequally yoked.

They had grown used to Charlie saying the prayers over the meals, so Kelli had never heard Carter actually pray. He was always respectful and usually added a hearty 'Amen' before eating, but Kelli didn't take that very seriously. She decided that she needed to discuss the issue of his faith with him.

She also wanted to ask him about going to church. She wondered if there was one close by, or only one in Emporia. She didn't think that Carter would want to drive all the way to Emporia every Sunday to attend church, even if he were truly a Christian.

Kelli picked up the Bible, slipped across the room and into the hallway. Outside of Carter's door, Kelli lifted her hand and knocked. The palm of her hands began to sweat as she nervously waited.

Carter strode across the room and pulled open the door, concern written on his face. Kelli had never knocked on his door before, and for a moment he thought that perhaps there was something wrong with Susan or Charlie.

"Can I speak to you a minute, Carter?"

"Is everything okay?"

"Yes, but there is something that I really need to know."

Carter stepped out into the hall. "Can we discuss it over a cup of coffee?"

Kelli agreed. "I still have a pot warm on the stove."

In the kitchen, Kelli poured them each a cup of coffee. Carter pulled out a chair and sat down. After his first sip, he set the cup on the table and gave Kelli his full attention.

Kelli had set the Bible on the table. She placed her hand on it for a moment and silently asked God for the right words.

"Carter, there is one thing that I do not know about you and I feel it is a very important issue."

"What's that Kelli?" She had his full attention now.

"I was wondering about your faith."

"My faith?"

"Yes, are you a Christian?"

Carter was silent for a moment. Memories of his angry outbursts at God when Abby had died flashed through his mind.

"Yes, I am a Christian. I just haven't been a very faithful one lately," he admitted. Kelli gave him her full attention. "When Abby died, I was very angry at God for a long time. It was almost impossible for me to accept that her death was part of His plan. But after a time, I began to realize that maybe it wasn't God's plan for Abby to live in Kansas or to be my wife in the first place.

If you remember, I told you that her parents basically forced her to come with them. She loved me, but I also think that when she married me she thought that she would be able to convince me to return east. She wasn't able to handle the harsh life here. I believe God's plans were really for her to stay in the east. Once I realized that it was Abby's parents who had taken her away from the life God wanted her to live, I no longer felt that I could blame God for her death.

When I met you, I was just beginning to understand all of this, and I haven't been sure just how much of my faith I wanted to show in front of you and Charlie."

Kelli reached out and placed her hand over his. "I'm so sorry that you have had to go through all this, Carter. When I am having a difficult time in life, I find comfort in my faith. However, I am aware that everyone responds to tragedy in different ways."

"I'm sorry that I've acted the way that I have. It was wrong for me to turn away from God, and it was wrong of me to cause you or anyone to wonder if I am a Christian."

Kelli smiled, glad that this issue was now out in the open.

"I wonder how you feel about me stepping into the place of spiritual leader in our family, when you and I are not actually..."

Kelli understood what Carter referred to but she assured him, "I would love for you to lead family worship and prayer."

"Thank-you, Kelli. I appreciate you bringing this up. I will begin tomorrow."

"That is wonderful, but we don't want to take the job of praying away from Charlie completely." Kelli smothered a small giggle with her hand.

"I wouldn't dream of it." Carter's eyes danced with laughter.

"What about church? Is there a church we could attend on Sundays anywhere?" Kelli asked.

Carter scratched his head in thought.

"The Welsh families have a Presbyterian church near town. Once a month they give a message in English, but other than that, no."

She was disappointed, but she did not want to ruin the camaraderie between them. "We could have our own family church right here," she responded hoping that she hadn't made him feel bad.

Carter nodded his head in agreement, he was actually looking forward to having a family church service. "I'll do some reading and be prepared."

Chapter 11

The next few days, Kelli was busy planning and preparing for her birthday picnic. Her feelings ranged from excitement to fear. She wanted her neighbors to like her, yet at the same time she was willing to dismiss them if they did not accept her because she was an orphan. She also worried how it would affect Carter's standing with his friends.

Two evenings before the picnic was scheduled, Carter insisted Kelli sit down by the fire after supper and relax.

"I would never have suggested this picnic if I knew you were going to work yourself to the bone, getting ready. The house is clean, the garden is weeded, the food is all made, and the tables are ready to be set up. Come and sit down."

Kelli stopped working, wiped her wet hands on her apron and then slipped it off and hung it on a hook beside the kitchen door.

"Alright! I suppose everything is as ready as it will ever be."

"Good!"

Kelli moved out to the large room and sat down in the chair across from Carter. She bent over to pick up a basket that had some mending in it, but Carter stopped her.

"No more work, Kelli. I mean it. You need to rest."

"A little darning won't hurt me," she started to explain, but the look in his eyes bode no argument, so she dropped the sock back into the basket and sat back with an exaggerated sigh.

"That's more like it." Carter smiled at Kelli. Her face was slightly pink from the heat of the kitchen and her hair was slipping loose from her braid. She looked adorable.

"I have a gift for you," Carter announced.

Kelli's eyes filled with wonder. "A gift for me? I would think a birthday party is enough of a gift for any woman."

Carter never ceased to be amazed at the selfless attitude Kelli had. At no time had she ever asked for any special treatment because she was a woman, and she by no means asked him to buy her anything beyond those items needed for cooking and general use in the house.

Kelli is a very special woman.

Recently Carter noted that he no longer thought about Abby all the time, but in this instance he remembered how Abby always wanted something extra. She had been very unhappy and discontented living on the farm, so Carter had tried to give her everything she requested.

Kelli would not even take the benefits from the things he had bought for Abby. Most of the items were either kept on display in the house for Susan to see over the years or they were carefully stored away in a hope chest for Susan. Carter had offered to give Abby's expensive dresses and other items he had purchased for his first wife to Kelli but she insisted they be saved for his daughter's future.

"A birthday party is not a gift, and this is not even the main gift I have for you." Carter reached under his chair and pulled out a small box and handed it to Kelli. "I just thought you might like to have this for the party."

With trembling hands, Kelli slipped the lid off the box.

Inside, on a pink satin pillow, was the most lovely brooch Kelli had ever seen. It was a white cameo.

"Oh my, this is just beautiful, Carter," Kelli glanced at it longingly, but then pushed the box back into Carter's hand. "I can't take it though. I'm sure its one of the things that should go to Susan one day."

"No, it is not. This pin belonged to my mother and I never gave it to Abby."

"Why not?" Kelli was surprised by the resolute tone in Carter's voice. He pushed the box back into her hands.

"I never felt compelled to give it to Abby. I think she might have laughed at me for giving her something so old. She would have called me too sentimental."

Kelli ran her hand lovingly over the brooch. "Why would you give it to me?"

"I thought that you would appreciate it Kelli; at least I hoped you would. If you would prefer a store bought piece of jewelry we can pick one out in town next week."

"No, I love this brooch. Are you sure you don't want to save it for Susan? It's not like I'm really your..." Kelli paused and dropped her eyes.

"Finish that thought, Kelli. It's not like you are really my wife. Isn't that what you were going to say?"

Kelli nodded.

Carter reached out and took Kelli's hand. "You are right about that. It was wrong of me to agree to marry you in name only. I should have courted you as Sister Marter suggested, so by now, you would believe me when I tell you that I do want you to be my wife; a real wife Kelli."

Kelli lifted her tear-filled eyes upward. Her smile lit up with joy. "Oh, Carter."

"I won't push you. I will continue to court you the best way I can, but when you are ready I want you to become my real wife, in every sense of the word. I love you, Kelli."

Kelli gently pulled her hand away, picked up the brooch and pinned it onto her dress. "Thank-you for the brooch. I will treasure it always." Kelli gazed at him with a look of pure rapture on her face. "I would love to say that I am ready right now to be your real wife, but I do think that we need time. Especially now that I know you want me as a real wife."

Carter stood up and pulled Kelli up from her chair and crushed her to him. He bent his head slightly and pressed his lips against hers. Kelli melted against him. After the kiss Carter stepped back.

"I plan on courting you, Kelli, so that you will want to become my real wife, but I also plan on courting you for the rest of your life. You have filled a place in my heart that I thought could never be penetrated again. For that I owe you so much."

"I don't need anything, Carter, and I don't want things. Just knowing that you love me and want me as a real wife is all I could have ever dreamt of having. I've prayed for this since the day we got married."

"I'm sorry it took me so long to realize my true feelings for you."

Kelli timidly leaned into him for another hug and then they sat down again and talked late into the evening, sharing more of their feelings with one another.

Chapter 12

The next evening, Kelli was so nervous about the party the following day. She felt exhausted, so she recommended that everyone in the house go to bed early.

"We all have a big day ahead of us tomorrow and we need all the rest we can get."

Charlie whined that he was not tired, but when Carter placed his hand on the boy's shoulder and insisted that he obey, Charlie reluctantly agreed.

"We can go out and check on Daisy together before we hit the hay."

"She wouldn't give any milk today."

"I know."

Charlie was very concerned about Daisy and Carter assured him that Doc Martin would be over for the party the next day. "He will check Daisy all over and tell us what's wrong."

When Carter and Charlie came back in, Charlie reluctantly shuffled off to bed. Carter turned and smiled at Kelli.

"I guess I need to follow."

"Are you upset that I wanted everyone to get to sleep early?" Kelli asked Carter.

He walked over and swept her into his arms. "Not at all, but I would rather spend more time holding my wife in my arms. "

Kelli allowed him to give her a long leisurely kiss, but finally pushed against him. "Enough of that. I need to get some sleep tonight. I don't want to meet all the neighbors with black rings under my eyes."

Carter laughed. "Okay, dear, but I'm really not tired."

Carter made his way down the hall and disappeared into his room. Kelli finished washing up the last coffee cups, then made her way to the room next door to Carter's. When she neared his open door, she heard his soft, even breathing. She was not even tired now.

Great, I'm the only one who can't sleep, she giggled.

Kelli tossed and turned, trying to get to sleep. She forced herself to lie still with her eyes closed, but nothing seemed to work, so she finally slipped out of the bed and wandered towards the kitchen for a glass of warm milk.

As she stood in the kitchen, heating the milk, she suddenly heard strange noises from outside. It was a sound unlike anything she had ever heard. She stood very still, listening, then stepped to the window and looked out.

It was dark, but there was a full moon so she could see the yard. At first she did not see anything, but she noted that the sound seemed to be drawing closer. She strained her eyes, trying to see what was out there. Nothing stirred in the yard, so she turned her eyes towards the fields. To her dismay, the whole field seemed to be covered by a huge black cloud. All of the sudden, Kelli jumped back as a bug landed on the windowsill.

Horror filled her eyes, as several more of the same type of bug landed beside the first. She had no idea what they were. They looked like grasshoppers, but they were huge.

176

Kelli grabbed her robe and ran down the hallway and stopped outside of Carter's room. Her heart was pounding so hard, but she wasn't sure if she should wake him or not.

Carter must have heard her feet pounding down the hallway. In just seconds he was standing up, holding her shaking body.

"What's wrong, Kelli?"

"I don't know, but there is something wrong outside. There are huge bugs out there."

Carter stood silently for a moment listening, then groaned, "Oh Lord, no!"

Carter ran down the hall and out the front door. Kelli followed behind. Carter was far ahead of her, making his way towards the field. She could hear him repeatedly yelling, "No Lord, oh please, no."

The bugs were all over the place. Several had already jumped up onto Kelli. She swiped at them, but noted that those that had landed on her dress, left small holes behind. They were actually eating the material of her dress. Kelli was horrified.

From the house, Kelli heard the terrified voice of Charlie. He was standing on the front porch.

"Kelli? Pa? What's wrong? What are all these bugs doing out here?"

Kelli ran to him. "I don't know, but you better get dressed."

Kelli heard the baby crying. She swept into the house. Susan was lying in her small bed with tears on her cheeks. There was one of the large bugs in her bed.

Kelli grabbed Susan and ran out into the hall with her.

"Where is Carter?" she yelled to Charlie.

"He's outside, trying to kill the bugs. I'm going out to help."

"Charlie, I don't think you can."

"I have to, Kelli." Charlie opened the front door and stumbled towards Carter.

Kelli wanted to follow, but she had to take care of Susan.

Kelli searched until she found a large basket. She grabbed several small baby blankets and put them in the basket and then she opened the front door and ran out with Susan and the basket. Carter saw them running towards him.

"Kelli, get back to the house!" Carter yelled. "Get the children back inside."

"We want to help." Kelli placed the basket down and put Susan in it. She covered the baby, and then put a blanket over the top of the basket. "What can I do?"

Carter looked at Kelli and Charlie. They were both determined to help. Carter turned back and looked across the wheat field. There was no hope for the fields now. The grasshoppers had already eaten their way halfway through the wheat.

"There isn't anything we can do now." Carter's shoulder slumped. He stood thinking. "There's only one thing that we can do, we need to save the red wheat seed." He turned abruptly and made his way to the barn.

Kelli picked up the basket with Susan in it. She and Charlie followed Carter, swatting off bugs as they went .

The barn was cold and dark. Carter lit a lantern.

"If we can keep the grasshoppers out of here, we will be able to save the wheat seed and replant next year."

"Will the grasshoppers go away?" Charlie turned fear filled eyes towards Carter. Carter pulled Charlie towards himself and hugged him.

"Yes, they are moving in a swarm. It won't take them long to ravish our field and move on."

"How can we keep them out of here?" Kelli pushed the basket towards the back of the Soddy barn.

"We need to start a fire in front of the barn, that will keep some of them out. The rest we need to keep raking up and throw into the fire." Carter explained. Kelli and Charlie listened wide eyed. "Kelli, we are going to need some ripped sheets to cover our mouths with."

Kelli ran back to the house and grabbed a sheet they could use. When she got back to the barn, Carter had begun to build a mound of dried wheat in front of the barn. He would use this to start a fire.

Kelli she tied a piece of the sheet around Charlie's head to cover his mouth. She handed some to Carter and tied one on herself. Carter skidded back into the barn and searched until he found two large rakes. He handed one to Charlie and headed out of the barn yelling back, "Kelli you stay in the barn. Come on, Son."

"I want to help," Kelli called out. Carter stopped in his tracks, turned and looked at his wife. Had it been Abby, she would have been in the house, hidden under the covers, but here Kelli was standing strong and bold offering to help.

"Are you sure about this? The grasshoppers could be here for hours and hours. It will be hard work. You could just take the baby inside; even in there you would have to fight them off some."

Exasperated Kelli insisted, "Carter, I want to help!"

Nodding in agreement, Carter stepped back into the barn and showed her the bags of wheat. "Find a broom and keep sweeping the grasshoppers away from this area. Don't let any of the bugs get onto or into the bags of wheat. This is our future. If we lose the wheat, we will lose the land."

"I understand." Kelli quickly looked around and found a broom. She could see that there were a few grasshoppers on the ground near the bags that had already slipped through the door. Carter had gone out front, but Charlie had not followed Carter, instead he stood frozen.

"Pa, the grasshoppers are on Daisy!" Charlie screamed.

Carter ran back to the door and looked in.

"I know, Charlie, but saving the wheat is more important right now. Come on outside with me, I need your help."

Kelli could see the worried look in Charlie's eyes, but he bravely nodded and followed Carter out to the front of the barn where they stationed themselves by the fire.

Kelli was kept busy for endless hours sweeping the grasshoppers away from the bags of wheat. She swept them into piles and every so often Charlie would come in and take the pile with a shovel out to the fire. Kelli noticed that Charlie's clothes had holes in them. Some from the grasshoppers and some from sparks from the fire.

"Oh, Charlie, your clothes."

A smudged face looked at her earnestly. "It's not important, Kelli, but saving the wheat is." Charlie made his way back outside with another worried glance at the cow.

"Please be careful," she called to him. In just a few short weeks, her little boy had grown up. He was so much stronger now and determined. Although Kelli was afraid for him, she was proud of Charlie.

Kelli returned to sweeping; hour after hour. At times she thought that she could not sweep away one more bug. Her arms ached with the effort, but she continued on.

Susan had slept most of the time, even though Kelli had to swipe the bugs off the blanket that covered the basket.

Once or twice Kelli was able to look out the barn door. Most of the time, the sky looked like one huge black cloud hovering over the fields, but after several hours she noticed the moon was beginning to peek through the black cloud. After five hours the bugs began to drift north. Kelli, Carter and Charlie continued to sweep, rake and burn for several more hours.

When the sun began to rise and the cow was crying, ready to be milked, Kelli was finally able to stop sweeping. Her eyes scanned the barn. Most of the wooden tools were destroyed. The bugs had eaten the handles. All the hay was gone. The cow's water trough was full of drowned grasshoppers. The only thing not affected by the attack was the bags of wheat seed.

Kelli dropped down and lay her head against the bags of wheat. Tears of exhaustion filled her eyes. Her hands were blistered and trembling. At least she had been able to protect the seed.

Just then, Carter pushed open the barn door. He and Charlie dragged in. They were covered in dirt and soot and their clothes were completely destroyed. Kelli quickly wiped the tears away. She could tell that Charlie's leg was hurting.

"I'll milk the cow now," Charlie bravely offered. Carter shook his head.

"It can wait. You've done enough, Son."

"Did we save the wheat seed?" Charlie asked.

Kelli stood up to reveal the untouched bags. "Yes!"

Carter looked around the barn and noted the water trough filled with bugs. "They got in here after all?" he moaned.

"Yes, I couldn't stop them, but I didn't let any get into the seed." Kelli could no longer stop the tears from flowing.

Carter stepped over and took her in his arms. She shook and wept. "You did great."

Kelli moved away from Carter to pick up Susan. "What do we do now?"

"I say we go see how the house fared. The bugs weren't moving in that direction, but you never know."

"I'll stay here and milk the cow," Charlie insisted. They knew he was tired, but he was also determined to do his job, so Carter allowed the boy to stay behind.

When they stepped out of the barn, Kelli was overwhelmed to see the damage. The fields were literally gone. The bugs had eaten every bit of wheat and grass as far as she could see. Kelli scrutinized the immediate area and saw that the bugs had also eaten the wooden seat off the buckboard.

As Kelli and Carter wearily made their way towards the house, they shuddered at the sight of the dead bugs; they were everywhere.

The front porch had some damage, but the house itself looked fine. Once inside, Kelli was dismayed to see that the grasshoppers had found their way in. Most of the blankets, sheets, clothing and curtains were all damaged.

Carter saw the tears in Kelli's eyes. "Not much of a birthday party after all."

His statement caused Kelli to consider her neighbors. "Do you think the grasshoppers ruined our neighbor's crops?"

"I'm sure they did. We can only hope that they by passed town. All the buildings there are made out of wood. The grasshoppers would have had a hay day there."

Carter sat down at the kitchen table. Kelli, still trembling from over-working her arms, laid Susan down to sleep in the bedroom, returned to the kitchen and put the water on to boil for coffee.

When Carter sat down at the table Kelli said, "I will have to make all new quilts for the beds."

Carter looked at Kelli. She was weary, but still standing. He was completely amazed.

"If the other farms weren't too damaged, the women will roust around, and help with the quilts. They have a special get together called a quilting bee. They invited Abby to join once, but she wasn't interested."

Kelli searched Carter's face. This was the first time she had heard him speak of Abby in a while. She looked for traces of sadness or regret. There was nothing there.

"I would love to join that group, as long as they can accept me."

"Why wouldn't they accept you?"

"Because I am an orphan."

"Kelli, you may have been an orphan before, but you are not one now. You are my wife and the mother of my children. We are a family, and besides, you were never an orphan to God. He has always been your father."

That thought had never occurred to Kelli before. Carter was correct. She no longer felt like an orphan.

"Where do we begin?" Kelli asked.

Carter shook his head. "The fields can wait. I won't be planting again until next year. Actually, the fields can be turned over now. I suppose I will spend the rest of the summer repairing the porch and all the tool handles."

Kelli nodded in understanding. "And I will be making blankets and sheets and curtains and clothing."

"That should keep us occupied until winter." Carter chuckled.

Kelli tried to imagine what it would be like in the winter. She had heard that the snow drifts were sometimes high enough to cover the house completely. It did not frighten her. They would be a snug little family. She actually was looking forward to that time.

While Kelli heated water for coffee, Charlie came rushing into the house, his eyes filled with tears.

"She won't give any milk," he cried.

Carter patted Charlie on the back and sighed. "I was afraid of that."

"What is wrong with her, Pa?"

"Hard to say. I told you that she was getting old." Carter tried to soothe the boy.

"Will she be okay?"

Carter squatted down and looked the boy directly in the face. "I don't want to lie to you, Charlie. I just don't know."

Charlie stared at Carter with anxious eyes.

"With her age and what just happened, it is hard to tell how an animal will react once there has been a natural disaster like this."

"Can't you do anything to make her better? We could rub some of the ointment you use on my leg on her."

Carter shook his head. "I'm sorry, Son, but that won't work in this case. Tomorrow I'll go to town and get Doctor Martin. He can come and check on the cow."

Kelli could see that Charlie was not relieved, but there was nothing he could do about it.

"Can I stay with her until then?"

Carter shook his head. "No, Charlie. I think it is best if you stay away from her until the doctor is able to tell us what the problem is."

Kelli turned a questioning eye to Carter. "Who is Doctor Martin? Lila mentioned his name when she visited here."

"He's the town doctor. But he also helps with all the animals on the farms."

Kelli set the coffee cups on the table and told them all to sit down. They bowed their heads while Carter thanked the Lord for protecting them during the grasshopper attack. Kelli could see that Charlie wasn't too sure that God had protected all of them.

After coffee, Carter, Charlie and Kelli all made their way towards their bedrooms. Kelli led Charlie to his room and tucked him under what was left of the blanket on his bed. She could see tears brimming in his eyes.

"Just get some rest, Charlie. Carter will get the doctor out here tomorrow."

"What if the cow dies?" Charlie sobbed.

"That will be very sad."

"You don't understand. If the cow dies, Carter won't need me anymore. He won't want to be my Pa."

Kelli's heart filled with compassion. "Charlie, Carter doesn't love you only because you take care of the cow. He loves you because you are his now. You are his son."

Charlie stared at her intensely. "Are you sure?"

"Yes, Charlie. Just like you and I are God's children. God loves us no matter what, right?"

Charlie nodded.

"Well, Carter is like that. He loves you no matter what."

Charlie yawned and smiled slightly. His eyes closed in weariness and he finally drifted off to sleep. Kelli stood up slowly and made her way towards the room she shared with Susan. She shook her head, thinking over what Charlie had been upset about.

When she reached the room, Kelli was surprised to see that Susan was still asleep. She bent over and touched the child's cheeks and noticed they were warm.

"You need to get some rest Kelli," Carter encouraged as he walked by the door.

"Susan feels a bit warm. She may be sick."

"You will not be able to help her if you are sick from exhaustion. Just lie down and sleep a while." Kelli sat on the edge of the bed and looked at her husband. He was so big, so strong and so dirty. He walked in and sat down on the other side of the bed.

"We are both filthy," she giggled.

"I know, but at least we won't get any sheets or blankets dirty, since there aren't any left on the beds." Carter chuckled, holding up the grasshopper eaten blanket that had been the cover.

Kelli couldn't stay awake a minute more. She lay down and fell asleep instantly.

*****

When Kelli awoke, the sun was high in the sky. She turned her head and saw that Carter was beside her, snoring. He must have fallen asleep at the same time she had.

Kelli's cheeks flushed at the thought of Carter sharing the bed with her. *That's just silly. All he did was fall asleep on one side of the bed.*

Kelli moved slowly, hoping that her movements would not disturb him. He needed the rest. He had worked much harder than she had, fighting off the grasshoppers.

Kelli stretched and walked over to the mirror. She was shocked at the sight. Her face was smudged with black soot and her hair was completely disheveled. Her dress had several small holes in it.

She looked over her wardrobe. All the dresses had a few holes in them where the grasshoppers had chewed on them. The blue calico, her favorite, was in the best condition.

Kelli padded down to the kitchen and quickly got some water. She made her way into Carter's bedroom and quietly gave herself a sponge bath, hoping that he would not hear her from the other room. Then she slipped on the calico dress. She spent some time brushing out her hair. She could hardly wait to take a bath in the river, but she knew she had to wait until Carter awoke and could tell her if it was safe to bathe there now that the grasshoppers had gone.

Kelli made her way back to the smaller room. She looked over at the cradle where Susan was sleeping. By now the little girl should have been fussing for her bottle. Kelli stepped over and picked up Susan. She was immediately alarmed. The girl's eyes opened but did not focus on Kelli. Instead, she drifted back to sleep. Kelli could feel the heat from Susan's body through the blankets. The girl's cheeks were bright pink.

"You have a fever," Kelli crooned.

She carried the baby out to the kitchen and settled her in the wicker basket she had used in the barn. Kelli found another old sheet that had many holes in it. She tore the sheet up and started to dip the strips into a cool bucket of water.

For the next hour Kelli applied the sheets to Susan's forehead. The child whimpered, but did not wake up.

Chapter 13

When Carter awoke, every muscle in his body ached. For a moment he lay still trying to understand why he hurt so much, then the memory of the grasshoppers flooded his mind.

He was glad they had been able to save the red wheat, but he knew that repairs around the farm would take endless hours. He was happy that he had Charlie to help him.

Carter rolled over and noticed that Kelli and the baby were gone. He pulled himself up off the bed and stepped over to the mirror. He was black from head to toe.

I've got to go and check the river right away, he thought. *We are all going to need to bathe, but I have to make sure that the water is safe. If enough grasshoppers died in the water, it will be poisonous for a while.*

Carter didn't even waste time putting on clean clothes. He couldn't see the sense in getting another set dirty.

In minutes, he was walking into the kitchen, hoping that Kelli had been able to pull together a meal. When he did not smell coffee or eggs cooking, his concern grew.

Kelli was bent over the basket, wiping Susan with cool cloths. She looked up when Carter stepped into the kitchen. Her face was streaked with tears.

"I can't get her fever down."

Carter rushed over and touched Susan's forehead.

"She's burning up," he yelled.

"I know. I wanted to take her down to the river, to cool her off, but I was afraid to go without you."

Kelli could see anger flash onto Carter's face.

"Why didn't you wake me up? Susan is very sick. She needs a doctor."

Kelli felt stung by his tone of voice.

"I thought it was just a little fever. I've nursed many children with fever before. I was getting ready to come and find you, however. I haven't been able to get her any cooler at all. She won't wake up either."

Carter stood up straight. Just then Charlie stepped into the room. He had been woken by Carter's voice.

"What's wrong Pa? Is it the cow?"

"No, it's not the dumb cow!" Carter pushed Charlie to the side. He reached for the back door. "I'll head to town and try to find the doctor."

"Should I come with you and bring Susan along?" Kelli asked.

"No, I don't want to expose her to the cold air. Just stay here and take care of her. That is what I married you for, isn't it?"

Carter slammed out the door.

Kelli sat stunned. She could understand that Carter was upset about Susan being sick, but she was unable to believe the words he had spoken.

Tears slipped down her cheeks.

"Kelli, what is wrong with Pa? Why is he being so mean?" Charlie asked.

"The baby is very sick. He is just upset." Kelli tried to assure herself of that, along with soothing Charlie, but in her mind the words kept ringing over and over again; *that is what I married you for, that is what I married you for.*

Waiting for Carter to return was torturous. Kelli continued to cool Susan off with the wet rags. She had Charlie help so that she could make some broth.

Once the broth was prepared, she dipped the corner of the rags into it and tried to get Susan to suck on the edge of the cloth. Susan did not respond and the broth dribbled down her flamed cheeks.

Kelli, picked the child up and sat on the chair by the table. She rocked the child and prayed repeatedly for God to heal the little girl. She looked over at Charlie and saw the fear filling his eyes once again.

"Why don't you go out and check on the animals?" she suggested. Charlie stood up, but hesitated.

"Go on now. I'll come out and ring the bell if I need you."

Charlie seemed appeased. He opened the back door and stepped out.

Kelli noticed that his limp was more pronounced today. He had been on his feet too long the night before, fighting the grasshoppers. She needed to look at his brace and make sure that it wasn't damaged.

The day slipped by slowly. Kelli didn't dare do anything except sit by Susan and continue to apply cool cloths to her face. She noticed her own stomach churning from hunger, but paid it no mind. She recalled that she was very dirty and needed a bath in the river, but that would have to wait.

Oh, Carter, hurry back with the doctor, she cried out in her mind, trying to still the memory of the harsh words Carter had thrown at her earlier.

After an hour, Charlie entered the kitchen. She could tell by the way his shoulders hung and the dejected look on his face that the cow was not any better. Charlie dragged his feet and slumped into a chair at the table. He did not want to burden Kelli, but it was hard to hold back the tears.

"Is she worse?" Kelli asked.

Charlie nodded. "She is lying down and she won't get up."

"Did you try to feed her?"

"Yes, but she won't eat." Charlie looked over at the baby.

"She isn't any better either?"

"No."

They both sat silently, side by side, for the next hour, waiting for Carter to bring the doctor.

*****

It had taken a bit of time to get to town and find the doctor. Luckily, so far no other farmers had called on him. Carter could see that the town itself was fairly undamaged by the grasshoppers, but he had noticed several farms, on his way in to town, that had been ruined.

When Carter told Doc Martin about Susan, he gathered a bag and followed behind Carter in his own wagon. He assumed that by nightfall, he would be in high demand if the fever that Carter's baby had, was something that was spreading.

Carter urged the horses to move as quickly as he felt he could push them, but it seemed as if they were making no progress at all. He tried to calm his spirit. He lifted up prayer after prayer, asking God to take care of Susan.

Carter wasn't sure that he could handle losing Susan, after losing Abby.

If I lose Susan, there will be no one left. His mind screamed, but then the image of Kelli and Charlie swam before his eyes.

He recalled pushing Charlie away from him earlier. Then the words that he had yelled at Kelli ran through his mind,

…that is why I married you.

Carter could hardly believe his own memory. He could not fathom what would have possessed him to say such a cruel thing to Kelli. He loved Kelli, and he loved Charlie.

Oh, Lord. I'm sorry that I was so mean to them. They have had enough hard times in their lives. They were so helpful during the grasshopper attack, how could I have treated them so appallingly?

*****

Kelli's head bobbed. She fought the need for sleep as she dipped the rag into the bucket of fresh water that Charlie had just given her.

Finally, she heard the sound she had been straining to hear all day; Carter's horse. Then she heard the jingle of a wagon and knew that Carter had found the doctor. Kelli laid her head on her arm and silently thanked God.

"Carter is back and he has the doctor with him," Charlie announced. Kelli stood up and tried to straighten her dress.

When the door swung open, she ducked her head, afraid to meet Carter's accusing eyes.

Carter stepped into the kitchen and headed straight to the basket. He bent over and touched Susan's skin. Kelli could see that he winced when he felt how hot she was. Kelli turned to the doctor.

"I've been trying to bring her fever down with cool rags, but it doesn't seem to be working."

The doctor moved towards the basket. He must have noticed how dirty Carter and Kelli were because he turned back before looking at the baby and suggested they both get cleaned up and rested.

Carter took this advice and headed out to the creek. Kelli would have liked to join him, but the tension between them was thick. Instead she offered to carry Susan back to the bedroom, so that the doctor could lay her on the bed and examine her.

As Kelli bent over to pick up the baby, Charlie moved out of the corner where he had been standing.

"Our cow is sick too," Charlie stated. The doctor turned back and smiled at Charlie.

"I'll have a look at her, after I see about this little girl." Charlie nodded in understanding and moved back to the corner. Kelli wanted to tell him to go out to the creek with Carter, but she knew that Charlie wasn't going anywhere until he found out about the cow.

Kelli left the doctor in the bedroom with Susan and made her way back to the kitchen just as Carter appeared, water still dripping off his golden hair.

"Kelli, you and Charlie can go to the creek. It is safe. The grasshoppers must have avoided it."

Kelli nodded. "The doctor is with Susan and he has promised to look in on the cow afterward," she said apologetically. "I know the cow isn't very important, but Charlie is concerned about her."

"That's fine." Carter sounded distant. "I'll just heat up some coffee and wait for the doctor."

Kelli called to Charlie to join her. He was reluctant, but obedient. Kelli and Charlie made their way to the creek bed.

Kelli was amazed at the damage the grasshoppers had caused, even away from the wheat fields. When they reached the creek, Kelli was glad to see that there weren't grasshoppers floating dead in the water. They both slipped off their clothing and spent the next ten minutes bathing.

The water felt so cool and refreshing. Kelli wished that she had just brought Susan to the creek. *Surely her temperature would have lowered if she could have been carried into the water.*

Kelli shook the water off of her body and slipped back into the blue calico dress. Charlie still had only his dirty clothes, so after he returned to the house, wearing those clothes, he would need another bath. Charlie seemed unconcerned about his clothes or being clean. All he wanted was to get back and hear what the doctor had to say about his little sister and his cow.

Finally, Kelli agreed with him and they made their way to the house. As they approached they noticed the barn door open.

"The doctor must already be in the barn," Charlie almost shouted. Kelli wondered if that meant that Susan was not really very ill. Surely if the baby were very sick, the doctor would still be with her.

Charlie wanted to join the men in the barn, but Kelli insisted he go and change his clothes. "We will have to throw away the ones you are wearing. They won't be any good anymore." Charlie rolled his eyes in exasperation. Clothing was the last thing on his mind. They both entered the house. Charlie ran to his room to change clothes.

Kelli slipped down the hallway and stepped into the room where Susan was still fitfully sleeping. There was a small bottle and a spoon on the dresser. Kelli picked it up. She was pleased. This was the medicine that the doctor in New York had given the nuns for the children who got very sick.

She bent over and pressed a kiss on the baby's hot forehead. Kelli was still concerned, because Susan did not respond and her breathing was very slow and shallow.

"Get well quickly little one," Kelli whispered.

Chapter 14

Kelli could hear the muffled voices of the doctor and Carter coming from the large front room. They must have returned from the barn. Kelli assumed the doctor was getting ready to leave, so she hurried down the hall. Just as she was about to step into the room she heard the doctor say, "No, I'm sorry Carter, there is nothing I can do for her."

Kelli stepped back with a small gasp, and held her hand up to her mouth.

"Nothing? What about the medicine?"

"I've left some, but there really is no medicine for what is wrong with her."

"Is she going to die?" Carter sounded so tired. Kelli's heart went out to him.

The doctor hesitated a moment and then said, "Yes, I'm afraid so."

Kelli could not believe her ears. She turned and ran all the way back to the room and flung herself down on the floor beside the baby.

No Lord, not Susan. Carter can't lose Susan too. Tears streamed down her face, her heart ached for Carter and for herself as well. She loved Susan.

Just then Charlie peeked into the room and saw Kelli crying. He walked over and patted her back.

"What's wrong, Kelli?" He bit his quivering lip.

Kelli had never kept things from Charlie before no matter how hard they were to hear or to accept. "I just heard the doctor tell Carter that Susan is going to die."

Charlie dropped down beside Kelli and turned saddened eyes towards Susan. "Not Susan," Charlie cried. His eyes brimmed with tears again. Kelli reached over and pulled him into her arms. They sat beside the small bed, slowly rocking one another and crying.

When their tears were all spent, Kelli straightened up. "Charlie, we mustn't say anything to Carter about this. He is probably grieving inside terribly. We won't make it any better by talking about it." Charlie nodded and looked at Kelli with his serious expression.

"Now Pa won't need either of us. I'm sure that the cow is going to die too." More tears dripped down the boy's face.

Kelli thought for a moment. What Charlie said was true. Carter had only married her to take care of Susan. He had been good and kind to her and Kelli thought they had even begun to love one another, but now that Susan was going to die, Carter would not need Kelli here anymore. There was no reason for him to continue in a relationship with her.

There was no doubt in her mind that Carter loved Charlie like a son, but she was another story. Still, Carter was a good man. He would not throw her out. But did she want to stay in a marriage with a man who did not love her? With a man who was tied to her for all the wrong reasons? Kelli's head dropped down to her chest. She gave one last long shuddering sigh. She stood up.

"Charlie, I know Carter loves you, but now he won't need me anymore. I don't want to stay knowing that he doesn't love me. He only marred me to take care of Susan."

Charlie nodded sadly in agreement.

"I think I should leave; go back to the orphanage."

"What about me?" Charlie asked.

"You can stay here, or come with me."

Charlie reached over and took her hand. "I'll go with you. I don't know if Pa loves me or not. When the cow is gone, I won't be able to help him much with my leg. I don't want to be a burden to him."

"We will leave tomorrow then. I can't stand to be here and watch little Susan die."

Just then Carter stepped into the room and saw Kelli and Charlie embracing. He felt awful for the way he had treated them earlier, but his fear for Susan's life had caused him to strike out.

Kelli noticed him standing there. She was silent.

Carter cleared his throat. "Uhm, Kelli. The doctor left some medicine for Susan." He pointed at the bottle on the dresser. Kelli nodded. "He said that there isn't much we can do, but try to keep her cool and give her the medicine."

It broke Kelli's heart to hear Carter explain the futileness of anything they could try to do for his child. She wanted to run across the room and take him in her arms and comfort him, but now he would probably only balk at that.

Charlie stayed beside Kelli and Susan the rest of the day. Kelli continued to apply the cool clothes to the baby and every few hours she would slip a bit of the medicine between the child's lips.

"Why are we giving her medicine if she is going to die?" Charlie whispered.

"It's probably just to make her more comfortable."

Carter had gone outside. Kelli thought it strange for the man not to spend every minute he could with his dying child, but she knew that people grieved in different ways.

She slipped into the kitchen and made a tray of bread and cheese to eat along with the broth she made earlier. She could not eat anything more than that. Her stomach turned with the heartrending thoughts of Susan's pending death.

In the evening Carter came in and moved lethargically through the house. He ate some of the bread and cheese but pushed away the broth. "I'm going to get some sleep. Wake me, if you need me to watch over Susan."

Kelli noticed Charlie's face, so full of longing for the father he loved. Kelli asked, "Are you sure about coming with me? I believe Carter would want you to stay."

"No, I want to go with you. God must have a different place for us. Maybe we were supposed to go back to the orphanage all along. That's probably why He didn't let me get picked."

Kelli gazed at the wise boy. "You must be right. I'm the one who pushed myself onto Carter. It wasn't God's doing."

Kelli insisted that Charlie go to bed. Once Carter and Charlie were both settled in, the house grew still and quiet. She moved Susan out to the big room in front of the fire place to keep an eye on her. Kelli sat in the chair and held Carter's Bible in her hands, flipping the pages and reading verse after verse hoping to find some comfort and relief.

I'm sorry, Lord, she cried out. I *shouldn't have pushed myself on Carter. I should have waited for Your leading. Please help Carter to be able to handle Susan's death. Help him Lord. Amen.*

Chapter 15

The next morning, Carter felt refreshed. When he passed by her room, he noticed that Kelli had not slept in the bed all night. He made his way towards the kitchen.

Kelli was slouched over in the chair, asleep. Susan was in the basket, sleeping. Carter moved quietly over and touched the child's cheek. It was still warm, but he thought that perhaps it was a bit cooler.

Kelli must have felt his presence, because she suddenly sat up.

"I must have dozed off. I'm sorry, Carter."

"There's no reason to be sorry. Susan is still asleep."

Kelli could see that the child's cheeks were still flushed, there had been no change, even though she had spent the whole night praying that God would heal the girl.

Carter could see how weary Kelli was.

"Why don't you go stretch out on the bed for a short nap? I'll watch over Susan. I can even scramble up a few eggs."

Kelli was surprised by his voice. He almost sounded happy. She decided that she must be tired. Of course Carter was not happy. His daughter was dying.

Kelli nodded. She needed to rest. She had a big day ahead. She had to figure out a way to get Charlie and herself back to town.

The sound of approaching horses nudged Kelli awake. She lay still for a moment listening. She heard the deep sound of Carter's voice. He must be outside and had already met whoever was out there.

It must be the doctor.

She pulled herself up and brushed off her dress. It was too bad that all three of her new dresses had small holes in them, but they were all she had now.

She slipped across the room and bent over the cradle. Kelli reached out a hand to touch the child's cheek but hesitated. It broke her heart to think of losing Susan, but until she could think of a way to get herself and Charlie to town, she would do what Carter had married her for and care for Susan.

Kelli turned and made her way to the kitchen, to gather up fresh rags and get a new bucket of cool water. It would be time for the medicine in a few minutes as well. As Kelli drew closer to the kitchen she heard Carter talking. He must have come in with the doctor.

Suddenly Kelli heard the soft trill of a woman's laughter. *Lila?* Carter's laughter rumbled. Kelli was shocked. How could Carter be laughing with Lila while his dying daughter lay in the other room? Kelli's face grew stern.

She stepped into the kitchen and Lila twirled.

"Oh, Kelli, hello."

Carter moved towards the door. "I have a lot of work to get to," he said and left.

"I just came over to see if my closest neighbors were alright. Carter tells me that he was able to save some wheat for planting next year."

Kelli swooshed around Lila and picked up a cup to pour herself some coffee.

"Yes. What about your farm?"

"Everything was ravished and the house is completely ruined." Lila's hungry gaze swept around the kitchen. "You are so lucky, Kelli. I am going to move into town. At least I will be closer to doctor Martin."

Kelli felt sorry for Lila, but maybe this was her chance.

"Lila, would you mind if Charlie and I rode into town with you?" Lila looked surprised.

"I thought Carter said that Susan was sick. Shouldn't you be staying here with her?"

"Yes, Susan is sick. I want to take her into town to the doctor. He wanted to see her again, and this way I can save him the trip." Kelli bit her lip, hoping that Lila wouldn't think about the fact that there was no one to bring them back out to the farm.

"Sure, you all can tag along with me."

"Thank-you. Let me just gather up some of Susan's things and we will be ready in a few minutes." Kelli scuttled out of the room. She rushed down the hall and woke up Charlie.

"We are going to town with Lila. We cannot take anything extra with us that won't fit in the baby basket or she will get suspicious. So get ready."

Kelli rushed to her room and gently spread the extra two dresses in the basket. She quickly wrote a note to Carter explaining why she and Charlie were leaving. She told him that she had taken the baby with her, so that Lila would not get suspicious, but that the baby would be with the doctor.

I am so sorry that Susan is dying. I would have given my life for her if I could have. But without your daughter you no longer will need me, so I set you free of any obligation you feel you have to Charlie and I.

Kelli fought back tears as she signed the note and propped it on the dresser. It was the right thing to do, even if it was going to break her heart.

*****

Kelli turned to look over her shoulder as Lila's wagon made it's way down the dusty road that led away from the house. Carter hadn't seen the wagon leave. She assumed he was in the barn working on new tool handles.

Take care of him, Lord, she silently prayed.

Lila chattered the whole way to town, explaining how she was planning to open a boarding house. She had hopes that some nice, eligible men would come along. Kelli began to wonder what she and Charlie would do about making money for the train fare. She hoped that there would be some kind of work they could do in town to earn the money, or they would just have to start off walking.

Kelli considered asking Lila if she would hire her, but Kelli decided to keep that as a last resort.

Charlie and I are both strong now, we should be able to find something to do.

*****

Carter set the tool down and wiped the sweat off his face. His eyes scanned the damaged barn and tools. He could see that he had a lot of work ahead.

I wonder why Charlie isn't out here helping me?

Carter ambled from the barn to the house. He noted that Lila's wagon was gone.

Good, it's time for me to sit down with Kelli and talk. I need to apologize for the way I have been behaving.

When he stepped into the kitchen, the room was silent. He was surprised that Kelli wasn't working on a meal. For a second his heart began to pound, maybe Susan was worse.

Carter rushed through the house and swung open the door of their bedroom. The room was empty.

Carter spun around and moved to Charlie's room. That too was empty.

Could they have gone to the creek? But as he passed by his room again, the note that Kelli had set on the dresser caught his eye. Carter walked over, grabbed the paper and opened it up.

When he finished reading it, Carter slipped down beside the bed.

Oh, Lord, what have I done?

*****

Leaving Susan with the doctor was not as easy as Kelli had expected. On his door there was a note indicating that he was away for a few hours.

"What are we gonna do, Kelli?" Charlie asked. "I'm hungry."

Kelli smiled weakly. "So am I." She berated herself for having made such a rushed decision. She hadn't thought about money for the train fare, or food.

If they went to the general store, they could purchase some items and put them on Carter's account, but Kelli shrank back from doing that. She still remembered the way the store owner had treated her. Kelli would have to get a job here in town to pay their way.

"Can we get some lemonade?"

Kelli decided that waiting in the small restaurant until the doctor returned was the best thing to do. They could order a glass of water.

"We can get some water, but I don't have any money for lemonade."

Charlie's head slumped. He remembered the wonderful taste of the sweet drink.

"We are orphans again, aren't we, Kelli?"

"Yes, but remember we still belong to God."

When they reached the small restaurant, Kelli asked if they could just sit and have a glass of water, while they waited for the doctor to return to town. The waitress assured them that would be just fine. She bent over and took a peek at the baby.

"She's got some pink cheeks."

"Yes, she has a fever."

"Oh, goodness. I'll bring some cool water for her as well."

The waitress returned quickly with a bucket of fresh cool water and two glasses of lemonade. Charlie's eyes lit up.

Kelli stopped his hand before he could lift the glass. "We don't have any money to pay for the lemonade," she insisted.

"That's okay, honey. I think we can spare two small glasses of lemonade today."

As she bathed Susan's face and sipped the lemonade, Kelli wondered if she might be able to get a job in the restaurant, or hotel. She had asked before, but maybe the girl the hotel had hired, hadn't worked out.

As Kelli pressed the cool cloth to Susan's cheeks, the baby gently opened her eyes. Kelli's heart stopped for a moment. She dipped the cloth into the lemonade and pressed it against the baby's lips. In seconds she heard the distinct sound of sucking.

"She's drinking." Charlie looked up, a pleased smile on his face. "Does that mean she is getting better?"

Kelli wasn't sure what it meant. "I don't know. I don't think that the doctor would have told Carter that she was going to die, if there were any chance she might get better."

"Maybe all our prayers have helped."

"We will have to talk to the doctor about it."

"What if Susan gets better? Will we stay then?" the look of longing filled the young boys eyes. Kelli shook her head.

"No, I should not have married Carter in the first place, just because he needed someone to raise his little girl. It wasn't God's plan. I pray Susan gets better, but even if she does, it doesn't change anything."

Charlie's shoulders sagged.

Kelli kept an eye on the front window where she could see the street. About an hour later, the doctor's wagon came rolling down into town. Kelli waited until she saw him pull up in front of his office.

207

Kelli stood up. "Come on Charlie, the doctor is back. We can take Susan over to him right now." She picked up the basket and they made their way down to the doctors office.

When they stepped into the office, the doctor looked up.

"Mrs. Hardy?"

"Yes."

"May I help you?"

Kelli felt foolish now. How was she going to explain the need to leave a dying child with the doctor? He was sure to think she was crazy.

"Uhm, doctor, I was wondering…."

The doctor stepped over and saw the baby in the basket.

"Oh, good. You brought Susan here. I was going to come out and check on her this afternoon. This saved me a trip. Can you please set her on the table over there." The doctor pointed at a long thin table where he usually gave his patient's their check ups.

Kelli flushed with embarrassment. She knew that she should explain to the doctor why she was really here, but instead she lifted Susan up and laid her on the table. She was surprised that Susan did not feel as hot as she had yesterday.

The doctor took some time looking the little girl over. When he was finished his examination he turned to Kelli with a grin.

"You've done a good job, Mrs. Hardy. The fever has broken and she is on her way to getting better."

Kelli's head shot up.

Charlie who had been sitting quietly during the entire check-up, bounced out of his chair. "You mean, she isn't going to die?"

"Die? Of course she isn't going to die. What ever gave you that idea?"

Suddenly the front door flew open. All three sets of eyes turned to see who was pounding into the office. It was Carter!

Kelli's face lit up at the sight of him. She was so glad to see him. She rushed to his side, but then she remembered why she was here in the first place. She took a step away from the towering giant.

"Carter, the doctor says that Susan is going to get better."

"I already knew that, Kelli," Carter stated. Kelli looked confused.

"How could you know that? We just now found out." Kelli asked.

The doctor interrupted.

"It seems that somehow your wife got the impression that Susan was going to die."

"I know." Carter acknowledged patting his pocket which held the letter that Kelli had left behind.

He and the doctor turned questioning gazes on Kelli. "What made you think Susan was going to die?"

Kelli stammered, her cheeks flushed. "I, I…I overheard the doctor telling you that she was going to die."

The room was silent for a moment, then Carter began to laugh. The sound rumbled through the room. Kelli turned and noted that the doctor was also trying to hold back his mirth.

"I don't see anything funny about that." Kelli stamped her foot.

Carter moved over and picked up Susan and cuddled her in his arms. "Kelli, what you heard was the doctor telling me that the cow was going to die, not Susan."

Her head shot up. "The cow?" she turned to the doctor for confirmation.

He nodded.

Kelli's cheeks flushed bright pink. She turned back to Carter. He was smiling down at the child in his arms.

"From what I can see, this baby is on the mend now," the doctor insisted. He shook hands with Carter and said, "I suggest you take your family home."

Carter glanced across the room at Kelli. Her back was ramrod straight. She was embarrassed by this whole situation.

Carter walked over and placed Susan back in the basket and whispered into Kelli's ear.

"Why don't we go sit down somewhere and talk."

Chapter 16

Carter carried the basket and led Kelli and Charlie back to the restaurant in the hotel. The waitress smiled and brought three glasses of lemonade. Charlie couldn't believe he was getting a second glass of the sweet drink in one day. He sat quietly, enjoying the drink.

Kelli sat with her hands folded on her lap, waiting for the tongue lashing she was sure that Carter would give. Instead, she found him reaching out and taking her hand into his.

"Kelli, I'm sorry that you thought Susan was dying. I wish you would have talked to me about it so that I could have clarified the situation."

Kelli did not look up. Carter cleared his throat, remembering the note she had left behind.

"Kelli, now that you know that Susan is not dying, are you still intent on leaving me?"

Kelli's eyes filled with tears, but she squeezed them shut, trying to hold them back. She nodded.

"But Kelli, why?"

"I shouldn't have married you just because you needed someone to take care of your baby. That isn't what God would have wanted."

Carter sat back. "How do you know it's not what God wanted?'

"God doesn't want people to get married just for convenience."

"But Kelli, I thought you loved me?"

Kelli was surprised that Carter knew that. She looked up at his handsome face and whispered, "I do."

"Then I don't see that God would have any problem with us being married. I love you too."

Kelli felt her heart ripping. She wanted to believe Carter, but the words he had barked at her when Susan was sick kept playing over and over,

That's what I married you for, that's what I married you for.

"You only married me to take care of Susan."

Carter moved his chair closer. "At first, that was true. But after a while, I really fell in love with you. I know I said those cruel words to you when Susan was sick. I regret them now. But Kelli, I really do love you. I love Charlie as well. You are my family now. Won't you please stay?"

"Do you really mean that, Carter?" Kelli gazed at him, hope refilling her heart.

"Yes. When I read your note it almost broke my heart. It was hard to lose Abby, but I promise you, Kelli, I would not be able to go on at all if I lost you and Charlie. Please say you will come home."

Kelli's heart was ready to explode. "Yes, oh yes, Carter, I will come home with you."

Carter leaned close and whispered to Kelli, "But this time I want you to come as a real wife."

Kelli's heart exploded with joy.

Charlie had been quietly listening, but now he stood up and whooped. "Thank-you, God!" Then he turned to Kelli.

"God really did have a special plan for us after all, didn't He?"

Carter pulled Kelli and Charlie into his arms. Kelli pressed her lips to Charlie's head.

"Yes, Charlie. God had a wonderful plan."

27594955R00116

Made in the USA
Lexington, KY
15 November 2013